96 HOURS

GEORGIA BEERS

Ann Arbor
2011

Bywater Books

Copyright © 2011 by Georgia Beers

Bywater Books First Edition: October 2011

Printed in the United States of America
on acid-free paper.

Cover designer: Bonnie Liss (Phoenix Graphics)
Author photo: Zoom'n Dog Productions

Bywater Books
PO Box 3671
Ann Arbor MI 48106-3671
www.bywaterbooks.com

ISBN: 978-1-932859-84-3

This novel is a work of fiction. Although parts of the plot
were inspired by actual events, all characters and events
described by the author are fictitious. No resemblance
to real persons, dead or alive, is intended.

To the wonderful people of Gander, Newfoundland. Thank you for opening your town, your homes, and your hearts and taking care of nearly 7,000 confused and stranded travelers on September 11, 2001. Your kindness and compassion are the very definition of humanity and you inspire this writer to be a better person.

Acknowledgments

It was a long, hard road taking an event as serious and devastating as 9/11 and wrapping a feel-good romance around it, but I had a ton of help guiding me on my journey and the result is something of which I am very proud.

First, thank you to the people at NBC who produced and ran their heartwarming documentary on Gander during the 2010 Winter Olympics. Had I not seen that, the idea for this novel never would have occurred to me. Also, thank you to author Jim DeFede, who wrote the book *The Day the World Came to Town*. It really helped me get a feel for details and specifics on what the stranded passengers went through that fateful day.

Thank you to the staff at Bywater—Kelly, Val, Marianne, Caroline—for not being afraid of this setting and for not trying to talk me out of this idea. Rather, you let me run with it and were incredibly supportive along the way. To my editors, Kelly and Caroline, you pushed and poked at me—and I wasn't always happy about it—but this book is better because of you. I am grateful.

Thank you to actress and philanthropist Erin Cummings, for your generous spirit and your dedication to and support of the LGBTQ community. You are the epitome of what it means to be a "straight ally," and I am honored to call you a friend.

As always, mucho gratitude to my dual sounding boards, Steff Obkirchner and Jackie Ciresi. My stories always improve after you two read them. Your two cents are worth *way* more than that to me.

Thank you to my dedicated readers. I'm so lucky to have such a loyal following. All the e-mails, the Facebook messages, the blog comments, and the attendance at appearances mean so much to me. A simple thank you doesn't seem like enough, but it's what I have to offer. I hope you never doubt my appreciation of your support.

And to my family at home—which somehow keeps getting bigger, no matter what I do—Bonnie, Mikki, Finley, Kallie, and Duncan: It doesn't seem scientifically possible, but you guys drive me crazy while helping me stay sane. Your love and encouragement keep me going and I'm so glad you're mine. I love you all.

Foreword

It's difficult for me to watch the news. There's so much fear and mayhem being covered that the occasional blurb of positivity is haphazardly thrown in as a fluff piece, such as coverage of a local dog show or a junior high school musical. It's as if the network knows that viewers have reached their maximum capacity for devastation and need to coast for a moment before hearing about another shooting or the outbreak of a different strain of the same illness we hear about every year.

It's as if America, despite the seemingly insurmountable issues we have to deal with on our own soil, is facing a new and more terrifying enemy across the ocean every year. Then again, with so many news outlets competing for ratings, I wonder sometimes if things really are that bad. Maybe. Probably. I hope not. Is it possible that this is just what is more interesting? Are the Democrats really so terrible? Yes, according to one news source. Are the Republicans responsible for everything wrong in America? Yes, according to another. Will you get shot tomorrow? Probably. Is it safe to travel outside of the country? Absolutely not.

And, to many, this endless stream of bad tidings has signaled the end of days, Armageddon, the rapture, etc . . . People say that things have never been as bad as they are now. Then again, I can't help but think back on Paddy Cheyefsky's "I'm mad as hell and I'm not going to take it anymore" monologue in *Network*, so beautifully delivered by Peter Finch. In that monologue, he talks about oil prices and the danger of leaving one's home—and this was a film that came out in 1976! People thought things were pretty bad back then, too! People thought things were pretty bad when both of the Kennedy brothers and Martin Luther King, Jr. were assassinated in the 60s. Hell, people thought things were pretty bad when Elvis Presley was allowed to gyrate on national television! So are things really that bad now? One could see it that way, but . . .

I can't imagine a better time to live than right now.

Despite all of the issues in the world, we are in a better position to understand one another than ever before. Pen pals can stretch to all corners of the world and communicate in an instant. Children are able to develop friendships and share their cultures, beliefs, and mutual fondness for Justin Bieber. Films and television shows from around the world can be shared, telling the stories of people who may not have had a voice before, thus raising awareness to social issues. For the first time in history, a black man and a woman hold two of the highest political positions possible. Women and people of color have more opportunities than ever before in history. And we are in the midst of a real, true fight for equality for the LGBTQ community.

This is an exciting time of change, much like the civil rights movement not that long ago, and straight allies stand beside our LGBTQ brothers and sisters. The movement has grown strong and the representation in art, film, literature and politics is greater than ever. Anti-bullying campaigns, support for No on Prop 8, and positive gay story lines on mainstream network television shows continue to educate people and support those who have been told that their lifestyle is anything other than "normal." I am so proud of and inspired by Georgia for her work in telling these stories of women, how they find each other, love each other, hurt each other and ultimately live their lives. They aren't defined by their sexual preference. They are people, period.

And, while there is still much to be done in the way of gaining acceptance and understanding, we have come a long way. The simple fact that you're reading this book right now is a testament to the sacrifices that many brave women and men have made and the risks that they have taken to have their voices be heard. I encourage you to lift your own voice, to share Georgia's stories of love and relationships and to be proud of your own stories that you create every day.

Erin Cummings

actress and philanthropist
ErinCummings.com & MittensForDetroit.org

September 11, 2001
Tuesday

Chapter 1

Erica Ryan had never fainted before in her life, but it felt like a distinct possibility. All of a sudden, the air in the plane's cabin had become stifling—thick, making her feel like she was breathing through wet gauze—and way too warm. She unscrewed the vent above her head, which released a weak stream of air that did little more than blow her hair into her eyes, and she quickly went from a little light-headed to alarmingly nauseous.

God, she wished she had the window seat. Then she could press her cheek to the cool glass of the window, maybe stave off the worry that she might throw up all over her way-too-expensive Michael Kors suit. But no. Instead, a middle-aged man with a donut of salt and pepper hair slept like a baby, as he had since takeoff, snoring softly in *her* seat, leaning comfortably against *her* window. She narrowed her eyes at him, hoping to glare him awake. He snored on, leaving Erica in the aisle seat. 33B. Worst seat in the world. She stretched her right leg into the aisle, just to be annoying, and wanted nothing more than to kick off her cursed heels, but she'd read someplace that it was never a good idea to remove your shoes on a plane. Something about feet swelling and shoes being tighter when you put them back on. She was pretty sure this pair couldn't possibly be less comfortable, but she wasn't willing to risk it.

It was hard to recall a worse trip. She hadn't wanted to go in the first place, but her boss insisted, said she was the right one for the job. She'd told him they weren't ready, that they needed more time, but he wouldn't take no for an answer. And how wrong had he been? She closed her eyes and tried not to think about all the work, the months and months and months of research

3

that were all for naught. She felt the beginnings of a headache in the back of her skull, the distinctive, maddening scratching, like little workers with picks poking at the nerves that ran down the back of her neck.

The flight felt like forever, like she was stuck in some episode of *The Twilight Zone* and doomed to be wedged into her uncomfortable seat for all eternity, fed only snack-sized bags of stale munchies and miniature cans of Diet Coke (certainly more edible than the "meal" she'd been served). How long had they been in the air anyway? She looked at the silver Cartier watch on her wrist—the best thing to come out of her last relationship—and tried to figure out how long she'd been flying, but she'd set it for New York time, couldn't remember exactly when their delayed flight had finally taken off from London, and trying to do the math made her head throb even more. She gave up with a sigh, wanting nothing more than to be home.

Tonight, you will be in your own bed. The thought floated around her head teasingly, but she seemed unable to grab on and, instead, swallowed down another surge of nausea, which left a bitter taste in the back of her throat.

Trying to ignore the sweat beading on her upper lip, Erica looked around at the passengers on the full flight and let her gaze fall on the brunette two rows up and across the aisle in 31C. Pollyanna—that's what Erica had nicknamed her in the airport because she seemed to be one of those people who elicited smiles and kindness from everybody who crossed paths with her. She was almost attractive, in a rumpled, beatnik kind of way; her dark hair in a haphazard ponytail, wisps of it escaping and doing their own thing, her jeans looking like they'd spent a day or two wadded into a ball and crammed into her backpack before being worn. On that backpack, she'd pinned an enormous rainbow button announcing her gay pride. Such billboard-like statements made Erica cringe and she'd tried to hide a disapproving grimace. Erica put her in her late twenties, maybe. She had watched her as they all waited to board. Pollyanna had chatted up a young couple with their little boy, then an older woman traveling alone, then the gay male flight attendant (aren't they all?). Each person who came in contact with her looked instantly smitten with her, including the African-American couple she was conversing with now over the back of her seat.

"You've been to London *seven* times?" Pollyanna asked. She must have been kneeling on her seat because her forearms rested on the seat back and she set her chin on them as she spoke to the couple. "Wow. That was only my second time. I loved it, though. I'll definitely go back." From this angle, her blue eyes were startling, framed by dark brows and lashes.

"Our dearest friends moved there about five years ago," the woman said to Pollyanna. "We miss them terribly and try to visit at least once a year."

"And now you're headed home?"

The woman nodded. "I love to travel, but I'm always ready to be back home."

Amen to that, Erica thought.

"What about you?" the woman asked Pollyanna. "You headed home?"

"Well, my mom works in New York and lives in Connecticut, so I'm stopping by to visit with her for a few days. Then I'm off to stay with friends in San Francisco."

"Why, you're just a traveling machine, aren't you?"

"I am!" Pollyanna laughed. "I believe in seeing as much of the world as possible. What's that old saying? A rolling stone gathers no moss? Something like that."

Erica rolled her eyes, then dropped her head into her hand and rubbed at her temple. The headache hadn't grown, but it hadn't receded either, and the pressure in the cabin wasn't helping matters. When she looked up again, blue eyes caught hers and held them for a split second longer than was comfortable. Pollyanna released her with a wink.

Before Erica had a chance to examine why she got a tingle from being caught by those eyes, the public address system clicked and the pilot came on.

"Ladies and gentleman, this is your captain. I'm afraid we need to make a slight detour. Nothing to worry about, no need for concern, but we're going to set down a little off our course. We'll begin our descent shortly, so please return to your seats. The flight attendants will be around to secure the cabin."

Confused murmurs washed through the cabin like a wave, people wondering what was going on. Erica could pick out snippets of questions that echoed the ones running through her head: Was there something wrong with the plane? What exactly did "a little off our course" mean? What aren't we being told?

Immediately wondering how she was possibly going to make her connecting flight if they were late getting to New York, Erica felt her earlier joy at the idea of her own bed slipping farther and farther away, fading into invisibility like a ghost. "God damn it."

She looked around her as the flight attendants scurried down the aisles like worker bees, pulling seats to the upright positions and collecting garbage. Every one of them seemed serious, concentrating, any expressions of good humor gone. Here and there, one would exchange an anxious glance with another.

"What's going on?" Erica heard somebody behind her ask. "Is there something wrong with the plane?"

"I'm sure it's nothing to worry about, ma'am." Erica craned her neck to see the flight attendant who'd been chatting with Pollyanna in the airport smile at an elderly woman a couple rows back. "You heard the captain." As soon as he had turned away from the woman, the smile fell from his face and his Adam's apple bobbed in a hard swallow.

Another flight attendant clicked on the intercom and told the passengers to buckle up. Nervous faces glanced around at one another and the murmur of puzzled and nervous conversation continued, a steady hum permeating the cabin. Erica saw Pollyanna reach across the aisle and pat the hand of the person sitting there, somebody Erica couldn't see. Whoever it was, they gripped the armrest of their seat so tightly, their knuckles had gone white.

"Don't worry," Pollyanna reassured them. "It'll be fine. The pilot knows what he's doing."

Really? How can you be so sure?

"Is your seat belt buckled, hon?" The flight attendant was looking down at her. His expression was kind, but his eyes still held apprehension.

"Oh." Erica clicked the belt. "It is now."

"Thanks. Great jacket, by the way." He touched her shoulder and moved on to the next row.

Snoring Man stretched his arms over his head and yawned like Rip Van Winkle. "What's going on?" he asked her.

Erica opened her mouth to answer when she felt the plane banking to the right. It really wasn't any less smooth than any other time the plane had made a turn, but because of the unease creeping through her body, it felt ominous. Her stomach did a flip-flop, reminding her that only minutes ago she was worried she might toss her cookies.

"Are you okay?" Snoring Man asked, touching her forearm. "You're really pale."

"I think so." *I hope so.* Erica swallowed down the bile that rose in her throat. *Yep. Definitely the worst trip ever.*

"Flight crew, prepare for landing," the pilot ordered crisply.

The flight attendants adjourned to their jump seats, so Erica could no longer see their faces, see if they still looked apprehensive, which was exactly how the rest of the passengers looked.

"What the *fuck*?" Snoring Man's voice was almost a whisper as he looked out the window. Erica followed his gaze, where she could see at least three other planes—in the distance, but much closer than she expected. "What the hell is going on?"

Erica wasn't the kind of person to get nervous easily. She was grace under pressure, a good man in a storm, all those stupid clichés, but this rattled her. Why were so many planes so close? In plain view? Were they getting some kind of escort in case they crashed? Good lord, were they going to crash? Was there something wrong with the plane and the crew just weren't telling the passengers to prevent all-out panic? Judging from the expressions on faces around her, others were following a similar train of thought. She could read them just as easily as if they were speaking aloud. *They say that the odds of being in a plane crash are long ones, but could this be it? Is my number up? Am I about to buy the farm? Kick the bucket? Bite the dust?*

Jesus, Ryan, get a grip! She tried to shake off the anxiety and settle her stomach, tried to steady her breathing and pick something to calm her nerves, an object on which to focus. She needed to calm the hell down.

Her gaze landed two rows up and across the aisle.

She couldn't see Pollyanna's face, she could see only the lower part of her jean-clad left leg and her left forearm and hand as it gripped her armrest just as tightly as everybody else did theirs. She wore a wide silver ring on her middle finger, and something about it held Erica's concentration. Pollyanna's fingers were slender, and Erica could make out the delicate blue lines of veins on the back of her hand, visible through the China-doll white of the skin. She forced herself to stare, to press all of her attention, all of her worry, onto that silver ring. As she did, her heart rate began to ease, her breathing began to steady, and the churning in her belly receded a bit. Long moments went by and she concentrated on the hum of the engine, listening for any noise that sounded suspect, but hearing none.

"Where the hell are we landing?" Snoring Man asked as their altitude continued to slowly fall. "It sure isn't JFK."

She looked past him and out the window, where the ocean was gone and she could see nothing but trees, trees, and more trees. "Jesus, is there even an airport?" she said quietly, more to herself than to her neighbor.

"I was wondering the same thing."

The landing gear came down, the loud noise jolting Erica, setting her heart to racing. She took a deep breath and returned her gaze to that silver ring, kept her eyes glued there, thankful Pollyanna was still holding tightly to her armrest. Erica's jaw was clenched and she consciously relaxed it.

Finally, after what felt like an eternity of nothing but forest, the never-ending expanse of green fell open and there was asphalt.

Blessed asphalt! Hot, black, bathed in sunshine. There really was an airport after all.

"Oh, thank god," Erica muttered aloud as the plane touched down, hard, roughly. Only then did she wonder if the pilot had been as nervous as his passengers. If there was a problem, he knew about it and still had to fly the plane. But at least they were on the ground. They couldn't plunge thousands of feet to their deaths if they were already on the ground. Erica finally pulled her gaze from Pollyanna's ring, rested her head back against the headrest, and blew out a huge breath as many of the passengers applauded. The nausea seemed to give up, deciding to pack it in and try another day. "Oh, thank god," she said again.

The mood in the cabin went from quiet fear to jubilation in a matter of seconds, people all around smiling and playfully wiping their brows. Erica took it all in, watching Pollyanna as she finally released her armrest and smiled at the person across the aisle from her. The PA clicked on and the captain spoke.

"Ladies and gentlemen, this is your captain again. I apologize for the rough landing, but we were told to land quickly. We've been advised that there is a national emergency in the United States and that American airspace has been closed. We'll give you more information as we get it. At this time, please remain seated. We're going to be taxiing for a bit."

He clicked off and the passengers were stunned. Erica and Snoring Man exchanged glances.

"National emergency?" she said after a moment of trying to absorb the pilot's words.

"We don't close American airspace," he replied with a shake of his balding head. "Ever."

As she looked beyond him and out the window, a completely different question took over her attention as she saw the block letters on top of the building they rolled past: GANDER.

"Okay, so where exactly is Gander?"

Chapter 2

"Ladies and gentleman, this is the pilot." Grumbles of annoyance rolled through the cabin; it had been hours since the pilot had given them anything but more bad news. "We've just been informed that we're next in line for processing, so it shouldn't be much longer." The grumbles changed to hesitant cheers. Nobody wanted to get too excited, just in case. "We appreciate your patience. Hang in there, okay?"

The PA clicked off and Abby Hayes drained the last of her third Diet Coke, not as smart a choice for her body since she didn't really need the caffeine, especially on a stomach that held only a small bag of chocolate chip cookies and some potato chips. She'd always been good at remaining calm, cool, and collected in any given situation; she was the one people turned to for reassurance in a crisis. But after being stuck on the plane—no, held hostage was closer to what it felt like—for more than five hours while they sat on the tarmac, went nowhere, and did nothing, she was just as antsy and claustrophobic as everybody else.

"A terrorist act in New York City." That was the only information they'd been given for why they'd been forced to land in Canada. Newfoundland. *Newfoundland*, for Christ's sake. She wasn't even sure where that was. Well, at least she could mark it off as a place she'd never visited before, add it to her list of travels.

"A terrorist act in New York City." She was sure a large percentage of the people on board kept coming back to those words. Abby did. She was worried about her mother. She was probably fine; New York is a huge city and the chances of the Metropolitan Museum being the place affected by a terrorist act were pretty slim. Still, she'd like to just call and hear her mom's voice, but nobody's cell could get a signal and the sky phones on the plane were useless as well.

Glancing out the window, she was amazed yet again by the sheer number of planes—and had the feeling there were more that she couldn't see. The airport was a virtual parking lot for jets. Every airline she could think of was represented. God, she wished she had more information, knew what the hell had happened. Counting nine planes just in her direct line of sight, she thought it had to be bad. Had to be.

The Bakers, the nice couple sitting behind her, also looked worried. Their kids all lived in New York and, like any parent, they just wanted to make sure everybody was okay. They had no way of knowing.

Abby stood up to stretch for the nine-hundredth time. The very broken-in jeans that had seemed like such a good decision for flying this morning now felt uncomfortable and constricting. Her feet were hot and tired of being stuffed into hiking shoes, her socks were too heavy, her ponytail was making her head itch, and she hadn't showered since the previous morning. She was not feeling her best and she was pretty certain she looked even worse. She fingered the peace sign pendant around her neck, sliding it back and forth on its brown leather thong as she scanned the crowd of tired, cranky passengers.

Most of those around her looked just as lost, anxious, and worn out as she imagined she did. The woman across the aisle who'd been so frightened during the landing had grown quiet, staring out the window over the lap of the younger woman beside her, whose nose was buried in a Stephen King novel. Mrs. Baker was knitting a pair of booties for her daughter, who was expecting next month. Mr. Baker's eyes were closed, but Abby suspected his thoughts were wide awake and on his children. Even the flight attendants were beginning to look haggard and exhausted, their attempts at servicing the passengers getting slower and more cumbersome. Jeffrey, the handsome FA she'd had such fun with since the airport, had lost the glimmer in his brown eyes. He'd seen the Gay Pride button she had on her backpack, had pointed to it and winked at her, then mentioned that he hadn't seen his partner in more than a week and was excited to get back home to New York.

Her gaze stopped at the gorgeous redhead two rows back across the aisle. Abby had seen her in the airport, and had trouble keeping her eyes off the woman. Her charcoal gray suit looked expensive and it fit her perfectly, the jacket caressing her shoulders, tapering in at her waist and following the lines of her body like a lover. The skirt was almost modest in length, hitting just above her knees, and the nylon-clad calves that led to black designer pumps were firm and smooth. Ivory silk was now fully visible, as the jacket was completely unbuttoned, which surprised Abby. Her hair wasn't exactly red—Abby didn't have the right word to describe it: sort of a cross between the brassiness of a copper penny and the deep cherry of an ocean sunset. Everybody else on the plane was rumpled and wrinkled, but not this woman. Every hair was still in place in the French twist (Abby wondered how long it actually was) and aside from the unbuttoning of the jacket, she looked like she'd just gotten dressed.

The only flaw in the design was the way she continually rubbed at her temple, her eyes shut—were they blue?—her manicured fingers working gently, rhythmically as she balanced her elbow on the armrest. They were signs Abby had seen in her mother ever since she could remember and she didn't stop to think, just reached into the overhead compartment and fished in the outside pocket of her backpack. She grabbed the water bottle from the seat pocket and took four steps, stopping to squat next to seat 33B.

"Hey, you look like you could use this." Abby handed over the water. The woman opened her eyes. Yup, blue. Icy and cold and blue. "And these." She dropped three orange pills into the woman's hand. "It's just Motrin, but maybe it'll take the edge off." At the lift of the woman's perfectly tweezed eyebrows, Abby smiled. "My mom gets migraines three or four times a month. Drink the water. It'll help." With that, she returned to her seat.

The redhead didn't like her, she knew that. Abby had caught her twice in the airport looking at her with thinly veiled annoyance. (Why? What had Abby ever done to her?) Then again on the plane, when Abby'd been talking to the Bakers, that same look. Abby had winked at her just to freak her out a little bit.

Something else: the redhead had pinged her gaydar in a big way. She wasn't sure exactly what it was—something about the way she carried herself. She looked fabulous in the suit, but it wasn't her usual attire, that much was obvious. She had an air of confidence, yet at the same time, she was uncomfortable, and that made Abby speculate on what her favorite surroundings were, where she was the most at ease. She wondered if the redhead knew Abby had pegged her and how much more apparent her dislike would become if she did.

Abby rolled her lips in and pressed them together, hiding the grin.

೦೩   ೦೪   ೦೩

The passengers were not allowed to retrieve the baggage they had checked, and that irritated the lot of them. They were told this as they deplaned and were corralled toward security.

"But, I've got important things in my bag," one man said to no one in particular.

An older woman looked worried. "My pills. What about my pills?"

Abby had traveled often enough to know to put an extra change of clothes and a toothbrush in her carry-on, so though she wished she could get her hands on her suitcase, she knew she'd be all right for a while. Getting through customs hadn't taken as long as she'd expected and as she followed the line of walking traffic, feeling a bit like a sheep, she caught a glimpse of red hair and a gray suit in front of an enormous map of the world. She walked up next to the woman and followed her gaze to the crude arrow drawn with a red marker. It pointed to Gander,

13

Newfoundland, on the very far eastern side of Canada. The words next to it said, "You are here."

The redhead stood quietly for a moment, sighed heavily, and muttered, "Terrific."

"This way, please, ladies." Before Abby had a chance to speak to the redhead, a kind-looking woman was waving them toward her and gesturing to a corridor. They both looked toward her and she smiled. "This way."

With a weary nod, the redhead adjusted her computer bag on her shoulder and followed the woman's directions, Abby just behind her. The airport seemed eerie and quiet and Abby wondered, not for the first time, exactly what time it was. Trying not to enjoy the view ahead of her too much—the redhead's ass was just as tight as her calves—she started to hear voices ahead. When they turned the corner, they were greeted by a congregation of people dressed in red-and-white vests and red windbreakers.

"The Red Cross?" the redhead said to nobody.

Abby stood and looked around. The redhead was right. It was the Red Cross. And if the Red Cross had been mobilized, they were certainly not going to be delayed for a few hours. It'd be a few days, at the very least. She looked around at the faces of bewilderment, wonder, and terror on those around her. Standing next to her, the redhead looked as if she'd come to the same conclusion as Abby and was now asking herself the same question: What the hell had happened in New York?

"This way, please. To the buses." A middle-aged man with a thick brown beard was gesturing to them much as the woman had at the entrance of the corridor. "Everybody on the buses."

Outside the airport, it had grown dark, but the air was warm and salty, a mischievous breeze rearranging hairstyles and toying with clothing. A fleet of yellow school buses waited for passengers. When one filled up, the next would pull forward. The scope of the operation amazed Abby, and she wondered how big this Gander was to have so many people ready to help.

"Where are we going?" the redhead asked the driver as they boarded.

"Your flight is going to the Lions Club, ma'am. It's not far." The driver was a man in his fifties, his gray hair thin on top, his blue eyes gentle. "Don't worry."

The redhead moved down the aisle to find a seat and Abby heard her mutter, "Is this Gander or freaking Stepford?"

Abby snorted a laugh. "I was thinking the same thing."

The redhead found a seat and Abby made a move to sit next to her, forcing her to slide toward the window. Once seated, she turned and held out her hand. "Hi. Abby Hayes."

The redhead eyed her and Abby could almost hear the internal argument. Manners won out and the redhead shook her hand. "Erica Ryan."

"Erica. That's pretty. It's nice to meet you, Erica."

"Ladies and gentlemen, can I have your attention for a minute?" The man who stood up at the front of the bus was in his mid-thirties and vibrant. His dark hair was tousled and his eyes showed kindness and sympathy. Once the passengers focused on him, he continued: "I know you're confused. I know you're tired. We'll be at the Lions Club in a few minutes and you'll be able to wash up, get something to eat, and rest. You'll also be able to watch the news on television. Now, I know a lot of you are wondering what's going on. Here's what we know: at around nine o'clock this morning, two planes flew into the World Trade Center in New York City." A rush of gasps ran through the bus like a swarm of hornets. The man held his hands up, asking to continue. "Those two planes had been hijacked in the air by terrorists. There were two other planes that had the same thing happen to them. One flew into the Pentagon. The other crashed in Pennsylvania." He allowed another moment or two for people to absorb what he was saying. Several people were crying. Erica and Abby sat stunned, as did the rest of the passengers. "The United States government immediately ordered American airspace to be closed, so all planes in the air over the States or en route to the States were ordered to land ASAP. That's why you're here."

Abby's stomach twisted painfully. She had friends in New York. She needed to know if her mother was okay. Several seats

15

up on the bus, she saw Mrs. Baker, her shoulders shaking, her husband trying to comfort her.

"As I said, there will be televisions for you to watch and phones for you to use to call your loved ones and let them know where you are." He paused and his voice dropped a bit. "When you see the footage, you'll understand why things were done the way they were." His throat moved as he swallowed. "If you find yourself in need of anything, please don't hesitate to ask. We want to make you as comfortable as we can while you're here. Okay?"

Abby wasn't sure how many people were still listening to him at that point. She suspected that most of them felt like she did: numb. Shocked. Confused. She turned her head to look at Erica, any thought of flirting or playing gone. Erica had the same thunderstruck expression on her face as she returned Abby's gaze. Neither said anything, they simply sat in silence for the remainder of the ride.

Chapter 3

The Lions Club reminded Erica of the local American Legion hall in the small Illinois town where she grew up and where her parents still lived. It was a large, rectangular one-story building, simple in its construction, yet housing everything a community might need for any type of fund-raiser or local celebration. She could almost smell the remnants of chicken barbecues and pancake breakfasts past.

The inside was broken into three large areas, plus a kitchen in the back corner and bathrooms opposite. Their flight had been full to capacity, so Erica estimated that there had to be close to two hundred people flooding the building. Conversation was at a surprising minimum, aside from the dozen or so overtired kids and babies who were making their dissatisfaction loudly known. Luckily, all families with children were ushered to the smaller area to the left. Those without kids were sent to the right. Some people went directly to the table in the lobby area on which sat four telephones. Others just meandered like sheep lost in a too-large pasture.

How was it possible that doing absolutely nothing for hours on end could make a person so damn tired? Erica wanted nothing more than to lie down in her own bed and sleep for three days. Her feet were killing her and the only reason she still wore her pumps was the fear of never being able to get them back on again. She'd almost sobbed out loud when they were told they couldn't get their checked baggage. She had a much more comfortable pair of dress shoes in her suitcase, as well as her Reeboks and three pairs of cushy athletic socks, for which her feet were now screaming.

Erica followed the expanse of people moving to her right, thinking absently that they looked like cattle being herded from one area to another. Okay, this way. Now this way. Down this hall, please. Onto this bus. Everybody too stunned to say much of anything or ask any questions, just doing what they were told. Once the guy on the bus had filled them in, they'd all pretty much been locked inside their own heads with their own thoughts and their own worries and no idea what was to come next.

The larger side of the Lions Club was obviously made for dinners and presentations. The tables had been pushed to one side in order to make room for the cots and air mattresses that now filled the other side like small boats anchored at a marina, lined up one after another for yards and yards. Her computer bag felt like it had gone from ten pounds to fifty in the course of a couple of hours and she dropped it unceremoniously onto the first empty cot she came to. Pollyanna—er, *Abby*—took the cot next to hers. Erica had been trying to ignore the fact that she'd been stuck to her like glue since the airport, so she said nothing. Abby had been right about the water and Motrin taking the edge off her headache, however. Erica supposed she ought to be grateful for at least that.

She was just about to sit when the TVs in the corner of the room caught her eye—two of them, back by the tables, on wheeled carts and turned slightly so as not to disturb the people on the cots. The passengers seemed to forget how exhausted they were, dropping their belongings and, like stray spaceships in the pull of a tractor beam, they moved slowly toward the televisions, toward the news reports showing on both of them.

The upper third of the World Trade Center's south tower was an inferno and fire shot from all directions from a plane that had flown directly into the building. People in the room gasped. Several began to cry. Erica barely registered anything the news reporter said. She just stared at the screen in horror and kept thinking, *This is some kind of sick and twisted hoax. This sort of thing doesn't happen in real life, only in the movies. It's a hoax. Right?* Then the second plane hit and any and all logic fled from her brain. Next to her, Abby grabbed her forearm and made a quiet strangled sound, startling her out of her trance. Erica turned and looked at her, saw unshed tears shimmering in her blue eyes.

Nobody said a word. The only sounds in the entire main room of the Lions Club were those emanating from the TVs and the mingled gasping and crying of some of the spectators. Everybody else stood stock-still, stunned, held captive by the footage they were being shown—people jumping to their deaths from sickening heights—unable to escape the shock of it all.

And then the south tower collapsed.

Exclamations of horror and anguish filled the air as they watched the building cave in on itself, like an aluminum can being squashed from the top down. Abby's hand flew to her mouth and her grip tightened on Erica's arm. Erica's breath stopped in her lungs—just stopped—and she felt a lump in her throat that she couldn't swallow down.

"Oh, god, all those people," Abby whispered aloud. "All those people."

Most of those watching were unable to move from the televisions, even though they wanted nothing more than to turn away, to wipe the images from their minds. By the time the second tower went down, nothing in the room could be heard over the combination of crying and swearing in disbelief. But after a few moments, there was a burst of energy, a stampede to get to the table with the phones, Erica and Abby caught up in the flow like leaves dropped into a rushing stream.

"Take it easy," a rotund man behind the table said. "Just take it easy. There's time for all of you to use the phones, but let's not trample one another, okay?" He managed to sound kindly rather than condescending and Erica wondered again if every resident of this little Canadian town was required to take Congeniality 101 or something as they grew up. If this many people had invaded her space, she'd be less than polite, she was certain about that.

Abby hadn't spoken since they'd left the TVs, something Erica found to be odd behavior for somebody who'd never shut up on the plane. She looked shell-shocked, moisture still pooling in her eyes and her face drained of all color. Before Erica could think about what she was doing, she grabbed Abby's arm and caught her attention.

"Hey," she said quietly. "Are you okay?"

"My mom. I need to get a hold of my mom. She works in Manhattan."

"Come with me." Without letting go of her arm, Erica pulled her away from the throng of people crushing against the telephone table and led her back to the cots. She rifled in her bag, pulled something out, and tugged Abby by the hand to a secluded corner. Once there, with Abby looking at her questioningly, she handed over her cell phone. Only a dozen and a half or so people on the flight had cell phones and they'd been swarmed by others begging to be allowed to use them. Erica had kept hers under wraps. Now, she simply shrugged at Abby's questioning expression. "I don't want everybody and their brother hounding me to use it. Call your mother."

Abby held Erica's gaze for a long moment before she took the phone from her hand and dialed her mother's house. When there was no answer, she tried again, her fingers trembling as she tried not to think about why her mother wasn't answering the phone at this hour.

Erica hung out in front of Abby, trying not to eavesdrop, but not wanting to move too far away and leave her open and visible to everybody in the place.

Abby hung up a third time and muttered, "I'm going to try her office." Erica simply nodded.

"Hayes. Michelle *Hayes.*" Abby spelled her last name slowly. The direct line hadn't worked and she was trying the main switchboard. It took her nearly a dozen frustrated hang-ups before she finally made the desired connection. Erica caught bits and pieces of the conversation, unexpectedly relieved to hear Abby finally talking about where she was and repeating over and over, "I'm okay, Mom. I promise I'm okay."

ର ଓ ର

On her way to the bathroom, Erica noticed a clock on the wall, round and industrial, like one you'd find in a school cafeteria.

1:17 a.m. She squinted at it, then looked at her watch, which read 11:47 p.m., Eastern Standard Time. She looked up again, then back at her wrist, as if the discrepancy would suddenly explain itself to her foggy brain.

"That one's right." The voice was kind, female, softly spoken. Erica turned to see the heavy woman with the graying hair who'd been wandering around the building since they'd arrived—a Gander native, apparently. She was gesturing at the clock on the wall.

"It is?"

"We're an hour-and-a-half ahead of Eastern Standard Time."

"You are?" *Apparently, I'm so tired I can't form a sentence longer than two words.*

"Yep. People always have a hard time wrapping their brains around it. We're actually the only area of the world in this time zone."

"That's weird."

The woman laughed, a hearty, deep laugh that made Erica smile despite her weariness. "My name's Corinne."

"Erica." She shook the proffered hand. They spoke quietly, since a good percentage of the people in the building were sleeping fitfully.

"Is there anything you need, Erica? Anything I can get for you?"

Erica looked around the lobby area, where rows of boxes and plastic containers held any kind of toiletry imaginable, along with donated clothing, linens, and food. *How about my suitcase from the plane? Can you get me that?* No longer concerned about smearing her mascara, she rubbed hard at her eye, her eyelid feeling like low-grit sandpaper. "No, I think everything I need is right here. I'm just going to go try to wash up a bit."

"Well, help yourself. Towels are in the bathroom. Don't hesitate to ask if there's something missing, okay?"

"Thanks, Corinne." Erica barely stifled a yawn as she took her leave.

"And try to get some rest."

Under her breath, Erica muttered, "Yeah, fat chance of that happening." In a huge room with more than a hundred strangers?

On a cot? In her suit? Probably not. Snatching up trial size packages of toothpaste, soap, lotion, and a toothbrush, she slipped into the ladies' room, relieved to find she had it to herself and knowing that wouldn't last long. Corinne wasn't kidding; there was a large pile of clean, neatly folded towels on the counter, used ones tossed into a couple of laundry baskets on the opposite wall. Seeing the variety of patterns and colors, Erica realized that these must have been brought from people's homes, collected by the local volunteers who were still making the rounds in the main part of the club, checking to see who needed what.

Studying her face in the large mirror, she groaned. She looked like hell, her hair doing its best to escape the clip she'd so carefully fastened this morning. Dark circles outlined her eyes and what makeup wasn't smeared was simply gone. God, what she wouldn't give for her flannel pants, ratty T-shirt, and falling-apart slippers. And a glass of wine. And a shower. But a glass of wine first. And if only she could take off her freaking bra! She'd looked damn good that morning for her breakfast meeting—which now felt like three days ago—when she'd donned her brand-new, six-hundred-dollar suit, but now she just looked like she'd slept in it. She might as well have. Wrinkles creased the jacket in strange places. The sexy clinginess of the skirt now felt like constriction instead. Her feet, still trapped in the godforsaken pumps, hated her with a passion and if she didn't get the pantyhose off in the next three minutes, she might very well have to kill somebody.

A middle-aged woman entered the bathroom, followed closely by a college-age girl. Both looked utterly exhausted, each smiling weakly at her reflection in the mirror.

When she finally exited the bathroom, she carried her jacket and pumps and tossed the stockings right into the nearest trash can. Her blouse was untucked from the skirt and her hair was hanging loose; she scratched at her scalp and almost purred. She knew it probably looked awful, but she didn't care. Padding along in her bare feet, a plastic bin caught her eye and she nearly wept with joy.

Flip-flops.

"Oh, thank god," she whispered, grabbing a pair of red ones marked with her size, separating them, and slipping them on. They were less than quiet and she tried to stifle their cheerful slapping, but she was so relieved to not be barefoot on public linoleum that she didn't really care.

A few insomniacs were milling around. Erica kept her eyes down, not up for chitchat. Some looked as wiped out as people who had just finished a marathon but couldn't now manage to relax. Some seemed utterly lost. Others looked panicked, all darting eyes and jerky movements. Erica put her jacket and shoes neatly on her cot near her computer bag, then glared at it, wishing now that she'd been more practical in what she'd chosen to keep with her on the plane. From here on out, clean underwear would always be in her carry-on. Always.

Abby's cot was empty, her beaten-up backpack sitting alone. Erica spotted her down the row, in a change of clothes that made Erica narrow her eyes in a moment of envy. She was sitting with the African-American woman, their heads close together, Abby's arm supportively around the woman's shoulders. Something about the pose, about the way they were sitting, made Erica's heart tighten in her chest and without thinking, she grabbed her cell and headed outside.

The night was warm. She'd heard more than one person during the day talk about how unseasonably gorgeous the weather had been, that it was usually quite a bit cooler in the early fall. The sky was clear now, stars visible to the naked eye. The salty smell of the ocean clung to the air and Erica inhaled deeply and closed her eyes.

On the insides of her eyelids, horrific images repeated: exploding windows and crashing planes and screaming people. She opened her eyes quickly, blinked rapidly to erase the visual, and dialed the phone.

"Hello?"

"Mom?"

"Erica! Oh, thank goodness. I've been calling your apartment, but you didn't answer. Did you get my messages?"

"No. No, I didn't. I'm . . . I'm not home." The relief she felt at hearing her mother's voice was so unexpected, it brought tears to her eyes. "My flight was diverted."

"But you're okay? You're sure? Oh, thank goodness. Did you see the news? Oh, isn't it just awful? What is this world coming to? You're sure you're okay?"

"I'm fine."

"Jim! Jim, it's Erica. She says she's fine."

Erica could hear the muffled sound of her father's voice in the background, the two of them talking over each other.

The phone changed hands and her father's gruff voice came on the line. "Erica? Where are you, baby?"

"Believe it or not, I'm in Newfoundland."

"Newfoundland? You mean in Canada? What the hell are you doing there?"

As she explained, she could almost see her father nodding along, listening intently to her. He'd always been a good listener, even when he was doing something else. He never babbled, not like her mother. He listened and nodded and used his words sparingly. She loved that about him. She pictured him now, in his jeans and flannel shirt even at this late hour, smelling like the outdoors. He would have taken off his baseball hat at this point, his graying red hair shockingly thick; he'd probably been sitting on the open front porch listening to the sounds of the night, sipping from his travel mug of coffee, ever present no matter what the hour.

"It's the strangest thing," he said quietly after they'd talked for a few minutes. "There's not a plane to be seen. I can't remember ever sitting out here and not being able to pick out at least four of 'em in different parts of the sky. Tonight? Not a one. It's just eerie."

His words made Erica lift her face to the sky and she suddenly wanted nothing more than to be there with her parents in Illinois, tucked into her childhood bed, the sound of cicadas chirping outside the window.

"When can you get home?" he asked, pulling her back to him.

"I don't know, Dad. I don't know when they'll let us fly again."

24

He grunted his acknowledgment of that, then asked, "How did things go on the trip?"

"Ugh. Lousy. Apparently, there are too many side effects. It was a big, fat 'try again,' just like I knew it would be."

"Aw, sweetie, I'm sorry about that. Well, you called it."

He was right, but that wasn't what she wanted to hear and she still ground her teeth at his words. She was a scientist in the research division of an international pharmaceutical company, heading one of their teams. She'd felt good about the work her group had done. In trying to come up with a drug to prevent migraines, they'd created one that at least took the edge off the worst symptoms more reliably than the drugs already on the market. Erica saw it as a breakthrough but needed more time to iron out some details. The company hadn't wanted to wait any longer, though, and sent her to pitch it to the U.K. division, against her better judgment. As she'd expected, they were worried about the severity of the side effects. Really, she had said, was a rash so bad if it allowed you to come out of the darkened, silenced room you were stuck in? Was blurry vision that big a deal? She knew how ridiculous she had sounded, had chastised herself about it but tried to remind herself she was just doing her job, doing what her boss had asked her to do. The problem was that the minor side effects got worse when the drug was used long-term, something she'd told him. The U.K. division had done a year-long study and when she'd flown to meet with them about it, they had given her the thumbs down. Of course.

"I did," she said with a sigh. "I guess I just hoped it would work out differently."

"Shake it off. Back on the horse." It was Jim Ryan's way of getting her to buck up, to not wallow. Always had been. Skin your knee? Shake it off. Back on the horse. Fail a class? Shake it off. Back on the horse. Broken heart? Shake it off. Back on the horse. Those words could really get under her skin at times, but tonight, they just warmed her inside and again, she felt the pull to be home.

"Thanks, Dad."

25

"Any time, kiddo."

She promised she was safe, told them she'd keep them posted, then hung up.

℘   ℘   ℘

"You really should try to eat something, Mrs. Baker." Abby held the energy bar out to her. "You need to keep up your strength. What good will it do you if you've fainted from hunger?"

Her weak joke was met with an equally weak smile, but somehow, she thought Mrs. Baker appreciated the attempted humor. She patted Abby gently on the knee. "You're a good girl, Abby. Your mama raised you right."

"You and my mama would get along great. Now eat."

She gave Mrs. Baker's shoulders a squeeze as her eyes registered Erica coming back into the room. She'd ditched the suit jacket and pumps—finally. Her blouse was no longer tucked into her skirt, her stockings were gone, and her hair was down. Loose and tousled, it was absolutely gorgeous and made Erica look younger and much more approachable. Whether or not that was the case remained to be seen, but she was devastatingly sexy and Abby itched to tell her so. Of course, as uptight as Erica seemed to be, Abby would probably get her face slapped for such a statement. Could the woman lighten up a bit? As she padded back to her cot, Abby could hear the flap, flap, flap of the flip-flops she now wore and couldn't help but grin at the overall picture. Erica turned then and caught her eye. And glared at her.

Serious was one thing—and given what had happened, it was to be expected. But Abby got the impression that Erica Ryan was always serious, that having fun wasn't high on her list of priorities. What a rough way to live.

She took her leave from Mrs. Baker and headed back to her cot. Erica sat on hers against the wall, eyes closed. She yawned widely.

"Ugh," Abby said. "I can't begin to imagine what she's going through."

A moment passed and Abby could almost hear the internal sigh, manners winning out again. Erica might have been overly serious but she'd been raised to be polite. "Who?"

"Mrs. Baker. Her son, Tyson, works at a brokerage firm in the north tower and she hasn't been able to get a hold of him. Nobody else in the family has either, so she's worried sick. She has no idea if he was able to get out in time."

Erica opened her eyes and looked in the Bakers' general direction. "That's awful."

"Do you have anybody in New York?"

She blew an auburn lock of hair out of her eyes and shook her head. "Thankfully, no. I wasn't even leaving the airport. Just changing planes and continuing on."

"To?"

"Raleigh."

"North Carolina. Great state. Love it there."

Erica closed her eyes again, leaned her head back. Abby wanted to ask her if she was from Raleigh originally, but knew she was tiring of the conversation. Still, she was happy she'd gotten her talking a little bit. She decided to ease up for now, though she had to make one more comment after scanning Erica's figure and stopping at her feet.

"By the way, I think the flip-flops make the outfit."

Well, I'll be damned, she thought as a ghost of a grin turned up the corners of Erica's mouth. *She can smile.*

September 12, 2001
Wednesday

Chapter 4

Sleep came fitfully and sporadically to just about everybody in the Gander Lions Club that night—if it came at all. Abby could usually drop off to sleep anywhere if she was tired enough, but that night, her mind was having none of it. At 4:47 a.m., she was still awake, her brain still racing. She continually tried to catalog the people she knew, wondering if any of her friends could have been in the World Trade Center that morning. She hadn't grown up in New York; she'd gone to school in Connecticut and her close friends and family were mostly there. But her mother had worked in Manhattan for almost ten years and she was bound to know people affected. Killed even.

Finally giving up on any kind of meaningful sleep, she sat up in her cot and looked around the darkened hall at her fellow passengers, wondered what was going through each of their minds.

A good portion of them were also awake—wandering, sniffling, sitting, staring. Mr. and Mrs. Baker had pushed two cots together and sat huddled side by side—trying not to think the worst and failing, probably. A young couple was walking up and down the aisles, an infant cradled and sleeping against the woman's shoulder. A middle-aged, balding man sat in front of one of the two televisions, though Abby wondered if he saw anything. The people began to blend into one another until they all looked the same: like aimlessly wandering souls condemned to some sort of purgatory with no idea what lay ahead for them.

Several of the volunteers were still milling around. Locals. Abby was stunned by their generosity. They'd brought food, clothing, linens, and toiletries from their own homes and had done nothing but smile, sympathize, and try to help since they'd arrived. Their patience with the tired and cranky travelers had been unending. She'd heard through various snippets of conversation that she had been lucky to get off her plane within six hours, that it had taken much longer for others.

To Abby's left, Erica slept soundly—or as soundly as one could sleep in a skirt and blouse on a strange cot in a large, over-populated room. She heard the comedienne Paula Poundstone in her head, doing part of a favorite routine: "She's such an angel when she's sleeping." Erica looked infinitely more relaxed. Her face was smooth, scrubbed free of makeup. Abby noticed a light dusting of freckles across the pale skin and smiled, figuring that Erica probably burned red as a lobster if she was in the sun for too long. There was no divot between her eyebrows from scowling, no lines at the corners of her eyes from squinting with suspicion. She looked utterly at peace. It was funny to Abby that she'd already concluded this was not a common expression for Erica. Some people were just that easy to read.

Realizing she was not going to sleep any time soon, she swung her legs around and stood. One last glance at Erica's work attire made her thank her lucky stars she'd packed a change of clothes in her backpack. She was sure she felt a hundred times better than most people around her, having changed into a pair of black wind pants and a royal blue T-shirt, but she could feel that hard-to-explain sticky feeling that comes from not having seen the inside of a shower in almost two days. Her scalp was itching like crazy, but she didn't dare take her hair down from the ponytail. Its flattened stringiness would test even her best I-don't-give-a-fuck-what-others-think attitude.

In the lobby area, two people were talking quietly on the phones, and the stocky woman with the silver bob who'd been present and smiling upon their arrival was still shuffling around, humming softly to herself. There was a crate of apples and bananas that hadn't been there earlier and Abby's mouth began to water almost instantly.

"Help yourself, dear. That's what they're here for." Her smile reminded Abby of a younger version of her grandmother, long dead but never forgotten, and the slight lilt to her voice sounded almost Irish.

"You're sure?" Abby kept her voice low, not wanting to disturb any of those lucky enough to grab a little sleep.

"Absolutely. You people can't subsist on bags of chips and cans of soda. That's not right."

Abby nearly swooned at the first bite of the perfectly ripened banana. "Oh, that's good. Thank you so much. My name is Abby, by the way."

"Corinne MacDougal."

"Mrs. MacDougal, you have been so wonderful. I don't know how we can thank you. You must be as exhausted as we are."

"First of all, it's Corinne. Mrs. MacDougal is my mother-in-law and I'd prefer not to be confused with her. Second, I figure it's the least we can do. My husband Tim is the president of the Lions Club, which is why we're here. Otherwise, we'd be at the high school or the legion or one of the other locations the passengers are being housed." At Abby's nod, she stopped what she was doing and asked pointedly, "How are you doing? Such an unbelievably awful thing. Are you all right?"

Abby blew out a breath. "I don't know. I'm trying not to think about it too much. My mom is okay, and that's the main thing for me."

"She's in New York?"

"Yeah. She said it's just crazy there right now."

"I can imagine it would be."

Abby dropped into a nearby plastic chair, feeling the need to talk and feeling that Corinne MacDougal was as safe as they came. "I just can't wrap my brain around it. I mean, who thinks doing something like flying planes full of people into buildings full of people is the way to make their point? What kind of logic says, 'If I kill thousands of people, maybe I'll be understood?' Why—?" She stopped in midsentence, embarrassed to feel her eyes well up, and she waved a hand. "I'm sorry."

Corinne laid a gentle hand on her shoulder. "Oh, no, Abby.

Nothin' to be sorry about, dear. It's a terrible, cowardly, tragic thing. You need to cry, you go right ahead and cry. I certainly did."

Abby cleared her throat, sat quietly, and willed her composure to return. "Cheer me up," she said, forcing a smile. "Tell me about Gander. Are you a native?"

Abby let herself fall into the gentle lull of Corinne's voice, the lilt almost musical. She unloaded fruit and set it out on the tables as she explained that Gander was a small town of just 10,000 people, a Super Walmart, an arts and cultural center, and a golf course. "I've been here all my life, born and raised. My husband, too."

"Do you have children?"

"One daughter. She's working in Vancouver, teaching at university."

"Vancouver, huh? It's gorgeous there. And kind of far away from here."

Corinne sighed. "I know. But she comes home every chance she gets and I go out there a couple times a year. Plus I have three sisters and a brother here and they all have kids, so I have a slew of nieces and nephews that I dote on. That helps with Kate so far away. What about you? Kids?"

"Oh, no," Abby said with a laugh as she shook her head. "No. Not yet. Maybe someday. Right now, I'm not sure I could keep a plant alive."

"Well, you're young, dear. You have plenty of time."

"Yeah. I believe in seeing the world, traveling all over the place before I settle down. *If* I settle down."

"Oh, you will."

"I will what? Settle down?" At Corinne's nod, Abby cocked her head, interested in her assumption. "How can you be sure?"

Corinne's hands stilled on the fruit and she grinned knowingly at Abby. "Isn't that what everybody wants eventually? A home and somebody who loves them living in it?"

"I never really thought that hard about it."

"You will," Corinne said again, still with the Cheshire cat expression, back to sorting fruit.

"I'm a little afraid of you, Corinne." Abby squinted at her,

34

feigning suspicion. Corinne laughed and waved her off. "So, how many planes were supposed to land here today?" A glance at the clock made her correct herself. "Er, yesterday."

"Tim says eight."

"How many actually landed?"

"Thirty-nine."

Abby blinked at her. She'd seen all the planes lined up on the tarmac, the Gander Airport looking for all intents and purposes like an airplane parking lot, but she had no idea there had been that many. "Thirty-nine?"

"That's what I heard."

"Holy crap. So, if there were an average of two hundred people on each plane . . . that's an extra, what? Almost eight thousand people!"

"Give or take, yep."

"Holy crap. Your town has almost doubled in population."

"That it has, dear."

"So, there are thirty-eight other places around town that look like this one?" Abby gestured the whole of the Lions Club with an arm, taking in all the people.

Corinne counted off on her fingers. "The high school. The community center. The golf club. The legion hall. Those are just here, locally. I know they bussed some passengers to other suburbs a little ways away because we were running out of room. Some went to Appleton. Some went to Gambo. Some went to Glenwood . . ."

"Wow." The scope of the entire operation boggled Abby's mind. She had to assume that the other planes were following the same rules as hers—specifically that nobody could get their baggage. That meant nobody had extra clothes or toiletries or any necessities they might have checked at the airport. And who knew how long they'd be here? Even with an extra outfit, Abby wasn't going to last long with no other clothing. And she didn't even want to think about how she'd smell tomorrow if she couldn't find a shower. The lobby space they chatted in now was brimming with supplies for the needy travelers: bins of toothpaste, toothbrushes, soap, shampoo, flip-flops, cereal, aspirin, bandages. Coolers overflowed with soda, juice, milk, and water. There were pies, cookies, and brownies that all looked home-made, spread out on one of the tables, fruit and bags of snacks on another.

The front double doors opened and a large man with white hair and wire-rimmed glasses wheeled in a handcart piled with boxes.

"Mornin', Corinne," he said cheerfully, as if it was not barely six in the morning. "Got some more things for your guests. And breakfast." He gestured to one box labeled "eggs."

"Hey, Bill. Bring 'em right on over here." Corinne gestured to the doorway of the kitchen and Bill followed her directions, the two of them chatting like these were the most normal circum-stances in the world. Abby yawned.

"Hey, there, Abby." Mrs. Baker laid a warm hand on Abby's shoulder. "Did you sleep?"

Abby snorted and swallowed the last of her banana. "Maybe ten minutes. You?"

"Nah. I won't be able to settle down until I know Tyson's okay. Do you think the phones are still working?"

"I'm sure they are." Abby walked with her to the tables and listened while she called her daughter and received the same news as last night: nobody had been able to get a hold of her son. Corinne had given her the direct number to the Lions Club, so Mrs. Baker rattled it off again and told her daughter to call as soon as she heard anything. At the worried and crestfallen expression on Mrs. Baker's face, Abby put a hand on her arm and squeezed.

"I don't know how much longer I can take this," Mrs. Baker said, her voice barely a whisper, her hands trembling.

"He'll be okay," Abby offered, unable to think of anything to make the poor woman feel better.

Corinne pulled up a chair and sat next to her, laid a gentle hand on her knee. "We're going to be shuttling anybody who wants to go to the Super Walmart to pick up some things later today. Maybe you should join in, take your mind off things."

"Oh, no, I think I'd better stay right here. I don't want to miss it when my daughter calls." She smiled apologetically at Corinne.

"Of course. I'll stay here with you then. Okay?" She patted her leg. Abby thought she'd never seen a kinder, gentler expression on anybody's face.

"When does the store open?" Abby asked. "It's not even seven."

"They're going to open it special for the visitors. They'll probably take people in shifts."

"I'll see if I can round some people up for the first one."

Corinne nodded her thanks and Abby felt a sense of relief that Mrs. Baker had somebody to sit with her. Over by the televisions, Mr. Baker was watching the news coverage; he seemed shaken and lost.

The young couple with the baby was still pacing up and down the aisles quietly. She explained the Walmart trip to them, then moved on to the woman who'd sat across the aisle from her on the plane, thinking maybe she'd like to get herself a new book or two. Then she hit the twenty-somethings that sat in front of her, the middle-aged couple across from them, and so on. By the time she made it back to her cot, the room was beginning to buzz with activity and Erica was just opening her eyes.

"Hi there, sleepyhead," Abby said, her tone gentle.

Erica managed a groan and rubbed at her eyes with the heel of her hand. "Jesus," she muttered. "This is the most uncomfortable thing I've ever slept on."

"At least you slept."

"You didn't?"

Abby shook her head.

"Not at all?"

"I just couldn't get those images out of my head. I was too wired or something. I think a lot of people had the same problem."

Erica looked around then, noticing how many passengers were milling about. She almost felt guilty for actually sleeping, but was distracted when the smell of bacon hit her full force. She was surprised she managed not to drool on herself, suddenly shocked by just how hungry she was.

"Oh, my god." Abby lifted her nose up like a dog catching a scent. "Do you smell that?"

"I'm starving."

"Me, too. Let's beat the rush. Wanna?"

Just as the passengers had been drawn to the TV the previous night, they all gravitated toward the kitchen like water flowing downstream. Abby counted six people in the kitchen cooking eggs, bacon, and toast, pouring orange juice, arranging piles of paper plates, plastic utensils, napkins.

"Where'd they all come from?" she asked aloud.

"Who?" Erica asked, arming herself with flatware.

"Only Corinne was here a few minutes ago. These Gander people are amazing."

Once they had food, Erica headed back to the cots. Abby looked around at the people sitting at tables. *Hmm . . . sit with strangers or follow the hot redhead?*

The choice wasn't a difficult one.

Her plate balanced on her lap, Abby filled Erica in on the trip to Walmart. "I could use some air. Want to grab the first shuttle?"

"To Walmart?"

"Yeah. Don't you need underwear? Some clothes?"

"From *Walmart?*" Erica's light eyebrows reached into her hairline.

Abby shrugged, took a bite of bacon. "It's your call. Get some pants and a T-shirt from Walmart or stay in your suit for who knows how long." She watched Erica's face, could almost hear her internal arguments, the listing of pros and cons in her head. "I'm sure there's a designer store around someplace. Or maybe a Victoria's Secret." She winked. "But who knows how long we'll be here, how far away those stores are, if we can get to them? Do you want to risk it? Do you want to be stuck in your monkey suit—nice as it is—for days on end?"

Erica looked down at her clothes, chewing her eggs and analyzing. What if they were allowed to fly today? She could manage for another half a day or so in these clothes, couldn't she? Shifting in her seat, she grimaced. The skirt felt like it had shrunk another size while she slept. She really wanted some clean panties and she was feeling sticky all over. Why did flying always make her want a shower? A clean shirt would go a long way in helping her feel at least a little bit better. But *Walmart*? Seriously? She would never buy clothes in one at home. Small kitchen appliances, yes. Picture frames, sure. But clothes? No. She had her reasons.

"At least come with me and take a look," Abby suggested. "You don't have to get anything. But just getting out into some fresh air will be good. The sun is shining. Looks like a beautiful day."

"What does it matter to you?" The question was out before Erica could censor herself and she tried not to look chagrined that she'd said it.

Abby looked taken aback for a split second, then reverted to the same ever-present grin and gave a half-shrug. "It doesn't. I just thought it would be good to get away from those news reports and the devastation a lot of us are feeling and focus on something else for a little while. I wondered if you thought the same thing. No biggie that you don't." She got up and took her empty plate to the garbage can that had been set up in a corner.

Erica had a hard time reading her. Had she hurt Abby's feelings or had it really not mattered? She couldn't tell, and that bothered her. The only thing she was sure of was that it suddenly felt a bit lonely without that stupid grin aimed at her—and she didn't like it. Blowing out a frustrated breath, she took her own empty plate to the garbage. Abby was chatting with a young woman holding a baby. Erica tapped her on the shoulder.

"Fine," she said when the blue eyes caught her and held her, damn them. "I'll go with you."

"Okay," was all she said, then turned back to the woman and continued on with their conversation.

Erica stood there for a minute, then felt a bit silly, so she meandered to the TV corner, where people seemed to be congregating once again.

Chapter 5

Erica was quiet on the bus ride to Walmart. Not that she didn't seem to be that way most of the time, but this was different. Abby studied her profile—the mole on her right cheek, the gently curved bridge of her nose, her full lips—and for some reason she wanted to know what was going on inside that head.

"Are you okay?" she asked.

"Yeah." Erica gave a quick, staccato nod, but continued to look out the window and didn't elaborate.

The school bus carted about twenty-five people down the roads of Gander. It was going to be another nice day, unseasonably warm according to Corinne. The sun shone brightly and if they didn't all know what had happened at home, it would seem like any other early fall day.

"So, Roy," she said, leaning forward in the front seat of the bus and addressing the driver; she'd introduced herself when they boarded. "You drive this bus all the time?"

Roy had salt-and-pepper hair and thick glasses. "Not this particular one, but yeah, I drive. Took the job after I retired."

"Nice way to make a little extra cash?"

"It's all right. Wish our employer would listen a little better. We're actually on strike right now."

Abby squinted at the back of his head. "On strike?"

"Yep."

"But you're driving now."

"Extenuating circumstances. We put things on hold when we heard you all were coming."

"All of you?"

"Yep, every driver. We'll go back to strikin' after all this is over."

Abby caught his eye in the rearview mirror and gave him what she hoped was a grateful smile. "Thanks, Roy."

"Hey, we're *all* Americans right now, hon."

She sat back in her seat and tried to fathom the bottomless hearts of the Canadians she'd met so far. She had no idea how she could ever thank them enough. Next to her, Erica hadn't moved, hadn't changed expressions, just continued to look out the window.

Despite the relatively small number of passengers on their bus, the Walmart was busy. Six other buses sat in the parking lot, spitting out passengers from other planes. It was the first time Abby really got a taste of the immensity of the situation. Gander had nearly doubled its population. How would it not burst at the seams?

"Okay, first things first," Abby said as she took Erica's arm and steered her.

They wandered through baby clothes and girls' jeans until they came to a wall of underwear. Erica wasn't sure if the swarm of women buying panties made her feel better or more self-conscious about her situation. She stood and blinked at the display, taking in the myriad of cotton panties—so many of them in pastels—and thinking about the lacy silk ones she had tucked at home in her dresser drawer.

"Hey, these are nice." Abby grabbed a three-pack of Hanes bikini briefs off the wall hanger. One pair of pink, one white, one light blue.

Erica snorted when she looked at the size. "I suppose I should be flattered you think my ass is that small." A woman next to her chuckled. Erica pulled a similar pack down, but in a larger size and containing panties all with brightly colored stripes. She walked away quickly without looking at Abby.

"Okay," Abby muttered under her breath, finding herself frighteningly turned on. "Stripes it is. Certainly nothing wrong with stripes. I'm good with stripes." She wet her lips and trailed after Erica.

If the underwear section was busy, the ladies' clothing section was mobbed.

Jesus, how long do these people plan on being here? Erica wondered as a woman hurried past her loaded down with what looked to be a week's worth of clothing. She stood there staring, not sure where to start or how, flashing back to her teenage years in a big, bad way.

Abby caught her deer-in-headlights expression and rolled her eyes. "Man, you're such a clothes snob."

"I am not," Erica protested, trying to sound indignant but achieving only whiny.

"Yeah. You are. Okay, look. You don't have to buy anything fancy and nobody at home has to know. Just get yourself something comfortable. Over here." She headed off to the right and Erica reluctantly followed her, stopping when they got to the athletic attire. "Here. It's nice out and all you want is to be comfortable for the next day or two or however long we're going to be stuck here." She handed over a pair of black Capri-length workout pants. "What about something like this? And a T-shirt or something? You've got the flip-flops or we could find some sneakers. Simple. Comfy. That's all we're talking about here, you know? It's up to you. Whatever you want to do."

Abby picked a couple of things off the rack for herself, her back to Erica in an almost dismissive manner; and for the first time in a very long time, Erica was embarrassed by her own behavior. Mentally taking a step back and analyzing the past ten minutes caused her to close her eyes and shake her head, to pull herself together. Moving closer to the clothing, she scanned the sizes and colors.

By the time they were seated again on the bus, they each had a good-sized bag filled with clothes that should get them through the next two or three days, if necessary. Both women hoped it wouldn't be that long, but of course, nobody knew for sure. The ride back to the Lions Club was quiet, Abby at the window this time, gazing out at the passing landscape. Erica tried to think of a conversation starter, but failed and opted for silence.

The Lions Club was abuzz upon their return, people excited for the next shuttle. Erica had to consciously keep from rolling her eyes over how easily entertained they'd all become after twenty-four hours stuck in one place. A bus ride to Walmart was going to be the highlight of the day for the majority.

Corinne was off to the side, talking with two men Abby vaguely recognized from the airport, though she had no idea where they'd been on the plane. When she glanced their way, Corinne smiled and gestured for Abby to join them. "Put your stuff down and come see me," she instructed. "Bring Erica too." Abby glanced at Erica and shrugged.

Corinne introduced the two men as Brian Caldwell and Michael Carr. Brian was around thirty with sandy hair and sad green eyes. He wore a Green Bay Packers baseball hat, jeans, and green sweatshirt. Light stubble decorated most of his face. Michael was in his fifties and dressed in a business suit, albeit a wrinkled one. His salt-and-pepper hair was slightly disheveled and he had dark circles under his brown eyes. His handshake was firm and his British accent charming as he shook hands with each woman.

"Okay," Corinne said in a somewhat hushed tone, which made Erica furrow her brow and Abby look around in confusion. "My husband Tim and I live alone in a rather roomy house. I don't know how long you poor people are going to be stuck, but we talked last night and we have room for four of you, if you'd like to get out of here."

The four of them blinked at her, not quite registering the offer.

"We've got two empty bedrooms upstairs," she went on, "and a sort of bedroom rec room in the basement with its own bath."

"Are you saying what I think you're saying?" Abby asked, a wary tone in her voice.

"Showers and beds. I'm offering showers and beds."

"For us," Brian clarified.

"I only have room for four and I've spoken to the four of you the most." She lowered her voice to a near-whisper. "But I need you to keep it kind of hush-hush because I really can't take everybody, though I wish I could." She looked genuinely saddened by this fact.

"You are the kindest woman I have ever met," Abby said with a grin, and meant it.

"Oh, I'm sure others are offering the same thing." She waved them off to get their belongings, telling them she'd let them know when Tim arrived to take them home.

"A real bed," Abby said quietly. "Maybe I'll actually get to sleep tonight."

"I was hoping we'd be out of here today. I want to go home."

Abby made a face. "We all do. But I think it's going to be another day or two. Have you checked out the TV reports at all? Things at home are a mess." They glanced over at the three dozen or more people who'd crowded around the televisions watching the coverage. "I still can't believe it. I can't imagine what it must have been like to be nearby and actually see it happening. The TV coverage is horrific enough, but to actually be there? To witness up close the towers coming down? The people jumping out the windows? My god. I can't believe somebody did this." She swallowed hard.

"I can," Erica said almost matter-of-factly as she sorted through her stuff. "I'm not surprised."

Abby stopped in midaction and stared at her in disbelief. "You're not surprised?"

Erica shook her head. "No. I'm not."

Abby studied her for several seconds before she issued a dismissive scoff and continued getting her things together. "Well, I am. Are you saying we deserved this? As Americans?"

"Of course not. That's not what I said. Nobody deserves this. I said I'm not surprised it happened, that's all."

"Seriously, Erica, it must suck to have so little faith in humanity. Wow." She noticed Corinne's subtle little wave and was relieved to have a reason to end the conversation. "Tim must be here." She shouldered her backpack, scooped up her Walmart bag, and headed toward the lobby without waiting.

"Damn," Erica muttered. Speaking her mind didn't often win her friends and admirers, but she'd learned to live with it. She told herself that Abby's dismissal meant nothing to her, that it didn't sting at all. Of course, she knew she was lying—and that bugged her even more.

Chapter 6

Brian Caldwell thought that maybe it was time to stop being a decent guy. After all, what had that gotten him? A cheating wife and a one-bedroom apartment, that's what. He'd been married to Carly for almost five years and she'd been unfaithful for at least three of them. He'd spent many, many months torturing himself by trying to figure out if there'd been more than the four affairs he knew about until finally his buddy Rafe smacked him upside the head. Literally.

"Bri. Enough, dude. Seriously. Let the bitch go. She took five years of your life, man, don't give her any more. Pull yourself together. Take a trip or something. Be a playboy for a few weeks. Find some tail and fuck your brains out. It's the best way to get through this kind of thing."

Rafe would know; he was on wife number three and only thirty-five. Brian loved the guy, but the last thing in the world he wanted to be was Rafe. Still, there was something to be said about sex with no commitments. He wasn't really that kind of guy; he liked having just one woman and being that one woman's one man, but he had needed to cut loose, at least for a while. Get his mojo back, restore his confidence, which Carly had shaken in a bad way. So he'd taken Rafe's advice and planned himself a three-week tour of Europe and it had been worth it. Anna Maria waitressed in a restaurant in Rome and Isabelle ran a bookstore outside of Paris. Each of them found his American accent enchanting, each of them rocked his world, and neither of them wanted any strings. It was the perfect scenario. Twice. He had no idea how he'd gotten so lucky, but he was about to return home a new man—or that had been the plan anyway. He'd wanted to be able to tell Carly to kiss his ass, but with all that had happened, a big part of him just wanted to be with her, to stand next to her and to hold her hand and to be outraged together, to mourn their fellow Americans. The rest of him thought, "Screw her."

Now he wondered if he'd ever get back into America.

He still couldn't believe it had happened. Fucking Middle Easterners. He never understood why the United States tried to bring peace to that part of the world. They obviously didn't want it. Leave them alone and let them wipe each other off the face of the planet, that would be the best solution. But now they'd struck on American soil, the bastards. Who did they think they were? Well, that was the worst move they could have made, killing thousands of Americans. They were going to be sorry. You don't go poking a bull unless you want to get gored by the horns, buddy. Simple fact of life.

Pulling his thoughts away from the mess back home, Brian focused on the present, specifically on those in the car with him. Michael seemed like a good guy. He was from somewhere outside of London and was traveling for business—on his way to Texas for a meeting, believe it or not. He was quiet and rather polite, though when you least expected it he'd toss in a zinger that left you blinking, wondering if he'd actually said what you thought he had. Abby was awesome already and he'd known the girl for only half an hour. She was charming, funny, and very friendly—not to mention hot. All that dark hair, the dark lashes, the dark brows and then those blue eyes. How could you not fall into those? Combined with the tall, lean body and killer smile, Abby made one hell of a package. Unfortunately, he wasn't her type; she'd made that pretty clear when she told him about her last breakup—with a girl—hoping to make him feel better. But hell, that didn't mean they couldn't be friends. He liked her. She was energetic and fun to talk to. Erica was much harder to read. She wasn't just quiet, she seemed to be inside her own head, not paying a lot of attention to those around her. The way her eyebrows dipped and formed a V just above the bridge of her nose told him she was always thinking. The suit told him she was on some kind of business trip. The way she sat in the car all tucked into herself against the door told him she didn't feel like having a conversation. She was just as hot as Abby (he had to admit the first time he'd noticed her had been in the airport the day before and that was because of her killer ass), but in a much cooler, much more unreachable kind of way. He suspected that she'd present a very large challenge to anybody who set his sights on her and wondered if he was up for it. Something to think about anyway.

"So, Tim," he asked. "What do you do when you're not carting around stranded airline passengers?"

"And bringing them to your house," Abby added with a grin.

Tim MacDougal chuckled from behind the wheel. He was a robust-looking man of average height and solidly built. Red-gold hair was losing the fight to silver and his ruddy complexion was tinted a light pink as if he was continuously blushing. Like his wife, kindness radiated off him in waves.

"I'm a high school English teacher," he said proudly.

"Did you take the day off?" Brian asked.

"Oh, no. School's closed for the time being. They've got more of you folks housed in the gymnasium and the cafeteria."

Brian shook his head. "I forget that there were other planes."

ભ ભ ભ

A couple moments later, two tractor trailers rumbled by them, heading into town.

"Looks like food," Abby observed, following the trucks as they passed, watching them out the back window.

"They're using the hockey rink as a giant refrigerator," Tim told them.

"Brilliant," Abby whispered in awe. She turned back around, her thigh pressed tightly against Erica's, whose gaze hadn't left the window since they began the ride. Again, Abby wondered what was going on in that beautiful head, but knew better than to ask. Erica obviously wasn't the kind of woman who thought about effect before saying what was on her mind, so Abby had decided to think twice before asking. Damn if the girl wasn't a lot of freaking work.

Not long after that, they pulled into the driveway of a modest, white, two-story house on a quiet street. The landscaping was simple and neat, pots of red geraniums adding splashes of color along the front walk and at the side door. The five of them poured out of the car and Tim popped the trunk so they could retrieve their belongings. One by one, they followed him into the house.

The MacDougals weren't rich, but they were happy and they took pride in their home. That much was obvious as soon the four guests set foot in the cheerful red, white, and yellow kitchen. Everything about it was bright, sunny, and inviting. Abby glanced at Brian and read the homesickness that was written all over his face, the sense of longing for his old life. Her heart ached for him and she patted him absently on the arm, hoping to offer comfort.

The vividness of the kitchen gave way to more relaxed and warm muted greens and gentle ivories as they followed Tim, single file, through the house and up the stairs.

"We've got two spare bedrooms up here and a guest bathroom," he told them. "You two guys can fight over who gets which room." Either one was a far better option than a cot at the Lions Club. Brian gave a nod of his head and a gesture toward Michael, respectfully allowing him to choose, then dropped his duffel on the twin bed in the second room and smiled at Abby. Tim gave them a quick tour of the bathroom and the location of clean towels, then said, "Ladies, follow me."

Back down the steps and through the kitchen they went, where Tim opened the door to the basement.

"When our daughter, Kate, turned sixteen, she told us she felt like she needed more independence." He rolled his eyes good-naturedly to show what he'd thought of that. "So, we converted the basement for her. Corinne and I called it the Inner Sanctum." With the chuckle that Abby was beginning to think of as his trademark, he hit the light switch and led the way down.

The MacDougal's basement was like a studio apartment minus the kitchen. Spacious and surprisingly bright, it boasted a wall of books, a treadmill off to one side, and its own full bath. A small sitting area with a loveseat, a chair, and a television was tucked into a corner. Kate MacDougal had been one lucky teenage girl—one who apparently liked the color peach. The walls looked creamy smooth and sweet, like sorbet, and Abby was tempted to lick one, like Charlie in the Chocolate Factory. A thick, rich cream carpet blanketed the floor and begged for bare feet, for wiggling toes. Cream and peach striped the shower curtain that was partially visible through the bathroom doorway and exactly matched the pillowy down comforter that covered the one queen-sized bed in the room.

"Yoo hoo!" Corinne's voice was sing-songy and cheerful, like everything else about the woman. She came down the stairs and stood next to her husband, a hopeful grin on her round face. "Everything look all right?"

"This is awesome," Abby said.

"Well, I didn't think the guys would appreciate sharing a bed, but you two are . . . friends, so I hope this is okay."

"We're not friends," Erica said.

"Oh," Corinne said. "I just assumed." Her ever-present smile faltered.

"It's fine. It's great," Abby said, willing her thanks to show on her face. "Please. Thank you so much for your generosity. You and Tim have been so amazing." She turned to Erica. "Haven't they?"

Erica blinked. "Yes. Absolutely. Thank you."

Corinne looked uncertain, but said, "I'm going to make an early dinner. I imagine you can all use a decent meal at this point. Three o'clock in the dining room. Everybody okay with pork chops? You two aren't vegetarians, are you?"

"I'm not," Abby replied, looking toward Erica.

"No." Erica shook her head. "Pork is fine."

"Terrific. I'll go tell the boys, then."

A couple quick gestures toward the linens and then Corinne and Tim took their leave, waving off Abby's continued thanks.

When they were out of earshot, Abby turned to Erica. "Are you always such a bitch?"

49

Surprise registered on Erica's face. "Excuse me?"

"They're being so nice. They're giving us a place to stay. You could try to at least pretend to be grateful. Jesus." She dropped her backpack and Walmart bag on the floor and looked around. It wasn't long before Erica's silence made her feel bad and she felt the need to fill it. "Sure beats the hell out of the Lions Club, huh?"

"Yeah. I suppose it does." Erica's eyes seemed drawn to the bed.

"What's the matter now?"

"Nothing. There's just, there's only one bed."

"Yep. But it's pretty big." Abby scratched under the rubber band in her hair, studied Erica, and barely kept from rolling her eyes. *Okay, time to mess with the Little Princess.* "Are you worried that I might attack you in the middle of the night? Try to have my way with you?" She waggled her eyebrows lasciviously.

Erica's head snapped around. "What? No. No, of course not."

"Ah. I see. You're worried that you might attack me."

"*What?*" Erica narrowed her blue eyes and a little anger twinkled around the edges. "That's ridiculous."

"Hey, I just call 'em like I see 'em."

"Don't flatter yourself. You don't know anything about me."

"No, I don't know a lot about you, but I'd bet my last dime you don't have a boyfriend or a husband at home. Maybe a girlfriend or a wife, but not a boyfriend or a husband. No."

Erica stood for several seconds with her mouth hanging open in disbelief, the expression so comical it made Abby bark out a laugh.

"Oh, please. Don't look so shocked. You pinged my gaydar the second I saw you in the airport."

Still at a loss for words, Erica just shook her head.

Abby rolled her eyes. "Don't worry. There are plenty of extra blankets in that drawer Corinne pointed out. You can have the bed. I'll be just fine on the loveseat."

"What—" Erica cleared her throat. "What caused the pinging?" At Abby's squint, she said, "I'm curious as to why you think you can label me so easily."

With a shrug—and trying hard to hide a smirk of victory—

Abby explained her reasoning. "Straight women love their clothes and heels, their makeup and pretty hairstyles. *Love* them. You don't. You like them okay, but you don't love them. That was my first clue."

"Well, that's a gross overgeneralization."

"And yet, totally true."

"Hey, I paid a lot of money for this suit and these shoes." Erica pulled her heels out of her bag and held them up as if they were the key evidence in a murder trial. "And I look damn good in them."

"I didn't say they weren't nice, that they weren't expensive. And I didn't say you don't look *fabulous* in them. I said you don't love them. You're a little uncomfortable in them and some of us can see that. It's no big deal. I hate them, too."

"I don't hate them." Indignation crept into Erica's voice, into her face, etching lines across her forehead.

"Okay. Okay." Abby held up her hands in surrender. "Whatever."

"What was the other one?"

"What?"

"You said my clothes were your first clue. What was the other one?"

"In the airport, you never once checked out a guy. And there were a lot of them there, but you never showed even an ounce of interest. Not once."

"How would you know that? You were busy chatting up every person with a pulse."

"And that was my third clue." Abby's victorious grin spread into a full-blown smile. "While you were pinging *my* gaydar, I was pinging *yours*."

"You were not." Erica grabbed her bags, stormed into the bathroom, and slammed the door. Hard.

Abby flopped onto the bed and tucked her hands behind her head. "I notice you didn't deny actually having gaydar," she mumbled, still grinning.

Half an hour later, Abby was dozing, her night of next to no sleep finally catching up with her. She jerked awake when the bathroom door opened, sending the scent of soap and citrus into the room, and tried not to let her jaw drop onto the floor.

Rude or not, uptight or not, Erica's beauty was not to be denied and the simplicity of her clothing made her look only more delectable. The Capri-length black workout pants looked made for her, snug against her body and accentuating what Abby was certain was one of her best features: her behind. The white T-shirt with cap sleeves was plain and understated and the red hair was still damp, wavy and falling to her shoulders. Bare feet with toes polished red topped off what was one of the sexiest visions Abby had ever seen. Not bad for Fashion by Walmart. Not bad at all. Erica glanced her way, drying the ends of her hair with a peach towel.

"Hey," she said.

"Hey," Abby replied as she sat up. "How was your shower?"

"Heavenly." Erica stood for a moment and nibbled the inside of her lip as if organizing her thoughts. "Listen, I'm sorry about earlier. I didn't mean to be so snippy. I'm just tired and I'd like to go home, you know?"

Abby nodded. "I get it. No big deal."

"Anyway. I tried not to use all the hot water. Better get to it before the guys do."

Keeping her shower considerably short was a difficult task for Abby; the hot water and soap felt divine on her body. She scrubbed her head viciously, loving every second of it while reminding herself that there were other people in the house who needed the plumbing. She was loathe to turn the water off, but forced herself to do so after only a few minutes.

"My god, it's amazing what a shower can do for your psyche, isn't it?" she asked as she left the bathroom.

Erica was sitting on the bed, looking over some sort of paperwork. Curled up by her bare feet was a gray and white cat purring so loudly Abby could feel it in the pit of her stomach.

"Who's that?" she asked.

"I have no idea," Erica said with a shrug, not looking up. "He just hopped up onto the bed and scared the shit out of me."

"He obviously likes you."

Erica shrugged again. "I like him."

Abby came closer. She reached out to scratch the cat's head, but he darted away. "Hey! Come back, kitty." She pouted like a child and plopped down on the bed. "I like kitties, too."

Erica kept her eyes on the paper in her hand, but Abby saw the corner of her mouth lift in the slightest bit of amusement.

"It's going on three," she said, glancing at her Mickey Mouse watch. "I'm going to run up and see if I can help Corinne with dinner."

"Tell her I'll be up in a minute," Erica replied with a nod. "I just need to finish this up."

"'Kay."

ଔ ଔ ଔ

Only when Abby turned and headed upstairs did Erica pull her eyes from her paperwork and look at her "roomie." She tried to avoid admitting to the fact that Abby was very attractive. After all, it didn't matter. Abby didn't really like her; she didn't really care for Abby. They had nothing in common and if they had to live together for longer than a few days, they might very well kill each other.

That didn't mean she wasn't fun to look at.

Abby's Walmart purchases had been much less extravagant than Erica's—if there was such a thing as Walmart extravagance. She had extra clothes in her backpack, so she wasn't as desperate as Erica. A pair of red gym shorts, a white T-shirt with a red maple leaf on the front, and clean socks and underwear. That's all she'd purchased. Her legs were undeniably sexy, lean and toned, probably from all the hiking she talked about doing. Their builds were quite different; Abby was slightly taller, her frame trimmer. Erica bet she stayed long and lean when she worked out, whereas Erica packed on muscle easily, definition appearing almost immediately after she settled into any kind of regimen. Abby was longer, slighter. Her hair was still damp and hung

53

barely past her shoulders, thick and dark. As she reached the top step, she quickly glanced back and winked one crystal blue eye at Erica, whose face heated into a bright red in a matter of a nanosecond at having been caught looking. Abby grinned and went on her way.

"Damn it," Erica muttered.

The ability to focus on her paperwork fled and she ended up staring without seeing it. So much had happened over the past three days that she was surprised she was still functioning. The disaster in New York City had come along and taken her mind off the disaster in her job. But now, she realized she'd rather focus on the disaster in her job than try to fathom what had happened in the Big Apple. It was too much to comprehend, so she chose to simply tune it out. At that moment, her intention was to never watch another news report about it. She'd just have to learn to focus on something else.

The cat came out of hiding and hopped silently up onto the bed, studied her with bright green eyes.

"How come you seem to like me?" she asked it. "I'm not terribly likable."

It stared some more.

"You got a name?"

It blinked once, slowly, then curled up between her feet, and lay down. The purring started up within seconds. Erica sighed. "Okay, then."

Hearing laughter emanating from above her, she picked out the individual tones of Abby, Corinne, and Brian, and she found herself smiling at the sound. Thinking about how she'd ended up where she was, how they had ended up where they were—four total strangers together now—she just shook her head. So strange. So very strange.

Where on earth did people like Tim and Corinne MacDougal come from? They were like characters from a fairy tale. If somebody had asked Erica last week about these circumstances, about the possibility of somebody welcoming complete strangers into their home for showers, dinner, and rest—out of the blue with no background on any of them—she would have laughed at the naiveté, at the sheer *stupidity* of such people. They'd probably be killed in their sleep—or at least robbed—by the very people they tried to help and they would have deserved it for being so gullible. That's what she'd have said.

And now? Well, she still thought they were naïve. But she was also grateful.

Another infectious burst of laughter came down the stairs—Abby's—and Erica caught herself grinning. Instead of listening from afar, she wanted to be a part of it, a feeling unfamiliar feeling to her. She put her paperwork away and headed upstairs.

Chapter 7

Corinne's dishes were white with bright red apples on them and reminded Erica of her grandmother's set back in Illinois, and as she scraped pork bones into the garbage she was hit by a sudden pang of homesickness. She handed the plate over to Michael, who rinsed it and put it in the dishwasher. The six of them had stuffed themselves with pork and potatoes and salad and had shared a coconut cream pie Corinne had made herself just a few days prior. Erica hadn't participated a lot in the conversation, but the evening had been pleasant enough and it certainly beat spending the time twiddling her thumbs, unshowered and stuck on an army-issue cot. She was thankful, that was for sure.

"Dinner was fantastic, Corinne," Abby said as she entered the kitchen, loaded up with dirty dishes, Corinne on her heels. "Thank you so much."

"Somebody's waitressed to pay the bills," Brian said as he gestured at the way Abby had plates lined up her arms, carrying several at once.

"I believe that any town in the world has an opening for a decent waitress," she replied. "It's hard work, but if you're good enough at it, the tips can be nice."

"I agree with you," Corinne said. "That's how I got through university."

"I tried waiting tables once," Michael said, his voice soft and deep. "The floor had a wet spot and when I stepped in it, my foot slid."

"Uh-oh," Abby said.

"I was able to stop my foot from sliding farther along the floor, but I was unable to keep the eggs from sliding clean off the plate and into my customer's lap."

"Oh no!" Corinne exclaimed.

"Oh, yes. My last day as a waiter, needless to say."

"I bet." Abby glanced at Corinne, who was cleaning things up. "Hey. No, no. We've got this. Shoo."

"You're sure?"

"Please," Brian insisted. "You fed us all. The least we can do is clean up."

"That's very nice of you," Corinne said, patting Brian on the arm.

Tim entered and looked at his wife. "Ready?"

"I'm going back to the Lions Club and Tim wants to help with some supply deliveries. You four are welcome to whatever you want or need. Food, television, whatever. Make yourselves at home, all right?"

"Liquor cabinet's in the dining room," Tim said, his face serious. "I imagine some of you may feel like a stiff drink after all that's happened. You go right ahead."

"I have no idea when we'll be back—I may just grab a nap there—so you just help yourselves," Corinne said.

"You're just going to leave four strangers in your house?" Brian asked.

Tim shrugged. "Yep." He winked. "Come on, love. We've got to get moving." With a little wave and a "toodle-oo" from Corinne, they went on their way.

"Unbelievable," Brian said.

"I think they're the nicest people I've ever met," said Abby.

"I think they're insane," Erica countered. Michael snorted a laugh.

"Why?" Abby asked, her face an expression of almost-hurt. "Because they're too nice?"

"Yeah. Something like that." While Erica certainly appreciated the generosity of the MacDougals, she couldn't see herself offering her house, her things, and all her private space to four complete unknowns. It would never happen.

"Well, I find it refreshing."

"I'm not surprised." Erica took a plate from her hands, scraped it, handed it to Michael.

"Not everybody hates people, Erica."

"That's true." Erica purposely avoided taking the bait, sensing she was getting under Abby's skin and enjoying the role reversal for a change.

"Hey." Brian stood in the doorway, unsmiling. "I don't know about the rest of you, but I'm totally down with what Tim said." He held up a bottle of tequila in one hand and a stack of shot glasses in the other. "Did I see some lemons in a dish someplace?"

Not taking her eyes off Erica, Abby nodded. "I'm in." Then she grabbed a lemon out of Corinne's fruit bowl on the counter and proceeded to slice it, bartender perfect, into small sections.

"Me, too." Michael tossed the dish towel onto the counter and headed toward the doorway.

It was the only time in her life when Erica recalled a shot of tequila sounding like anything but dangerous. She wasn't somebody who drank often; she didn't like feeling out of control. But this was different somehow. She scooped up the salt shaker and followed the trio into the dining room.

Like the kitchen, nothing in the dining room was obviously expensive, but it was all nice, neat, and coordinated. A hutch sat along the back wall and displayed a set of china with a subtle daylily design on it. The table was small, but they'd added a leaf and Tim had pulled extra chairs from someplace upstairs so there'd be room for all of them at dinner. They took the same seats they'd had then and looked at one another.

None of them really wanted to talk about the towers, about the hijackings, about the loss of life and the blow to the confidence and safety of all Americans, but those were the elephants in the room and once addressed, the foursome couldn't stop. And the more they talked, the angrier they became. And the angrier they became, the more they drank. By the third round of shots, Abby and Brian were both in tears. Erica was staring into her glass, wishing she were someplace else talking about anything else. Michael was just as horrified as the rest of them.

"I fly to Texas for my job six, sometimes seven times a year. America is my home away from home. I cannot fathom somebody doing this. I just can't. It's appalling. Abhorrent. It makes me physically ill."

"Okay." Brian took a deep breath. "Okay. I've had enough. Can we talk about something else? What about you guys? Tell me about all of you." He looked around the table, his green eyes boring into each of them. "You're the people I'm with at this moment. This is our JFK moment, you know? It's like how everybody who was around in the '60s can tell you exactly where they were and what they were doing when they heard that Kennedy was shot. This is our version of that. I will always remember where I was and what I was doing—and you. I will always remember you guys and I want to know more." His words trailed off, frayed by alcohol and emotion.

"I know! Hold that thought." Abby jumped up and left the room abruptly.

"I have no idea," Erica said with a shrug when both men looked expectantly at her.

They sat quietly, each lost in thought, looking around the dining room of the strangers who'd been so kind. Brian's gaze fell on a small red book on an end table and he picked it up, began thumbing through the pages.

Abby returned with a square blue box. "I saw this on one of the shelves downstairs."

"Yahtzee?" Erica asked. "Seriously?"

A flash of hurt zipped across Abby's face. "I thought it would help us bond. What's more American than the game of Yahtzee?"

Erica had no comeback for that. Instead, she helped open up the box. "If we're playing Yahtzee, I'm going to need another shot," she said to Brian, whose face was still in the book. "What's that?" Craning her neck to see the cover, she read, "'If. Five hundred questions for the game of life.'"

Abby handed everybody a score sheet and explained the rules. Taking the dice out, she handed each person one and said, "Highest roll goes first." She then proceeded to roll herself a six.

"Of course," Erica muttered.

"Wait." Brian looked at the dice, then at the book in his hand, then back at the dice, a smile forming on his lips. "I've got a better idea. A way we can get to know each other. And maybe take our minds off this shit for a little while." He picked up two dice and rolled them. A four and a six. "Page forty-six." He flipped to that page, and read. "If you could rid the earth of one thing, what would it be?"

Erica hated this game already.

"Well, hell," Brian went on, answering his own question. "That's easy. Fucking crazy Middle Eastern terrorists. Duh." His smile was forced and the anger in his eyes was nearly palpable.

"Not exactly taking my mind off it," Michael stated. "I don't know about the rest of you."

"No, if we're going to do this," Abby said, the wheels in her mind turning, "we have to do it in an organized manner. We can't just be blurting out questions." She grabbed the dice. "I'm one, Erica's two, Michael is three, and Brian is four. We'll roll one die to decide who gets to answer—just roll again if you get a five or six. We'll roll both dice to choose the page number of the book, like Brian just did. The reader can choose any question on that page. Capisce?"

Brian nodded. Michael and Erica just blinked.

"I'll start," Abby replied, not waiting for a response and rolling a die. "Three. Michael." She rolled for the page, studied the questions, and smiled. "Okay. If you had to choose the single most charming person you've ever met, who would it be?"

Michael didn't need to think long. "I'd say Corinne's right up there at the top."

Nods surged around the table. "I'll drink to that," Brian said, lifting his glass. They cheered and downed the shooters.

"Hoo," Erica said, closing her eyes momentarily. "I'm going to have to graduate to sipping from now on." The world around her swam out of focus for a second, then cleared.

The dice and book went to Michael, who rolled Brian's number. "If you could own one article of clothing from any film, what would you take?"

"Oh, that's a good one," Erica said. Abby agreed.

"I'd have to say . . ." Brian scratched his chin. "I'd have to say Bogie's hat from *Casablanca*. Coolest hat ever."

"Good choice," Abby commended him, then turned her crystal blue gaze on Erica. "What would you have said?"

"Lara Croft's entire tomb-raiding outfit," she replied without missing a beat.

"Complete with guns?" Abby asked, arching an eyebrow.

"Complete with guns."

"And would you actually wear it?"

"Absolutely."

"You'd look hot."

"Damn right I would." Erica could feel the guys watching them, but the tequila told her she didn't care.

"Brian," Abby said after a moment of holding Erica's gaze. "Your turn."

He rolled Erica's number, scanned the page, and grinned wickedly. "If you were to become a prostitute, how much money do you think you could charge per hour?"

"Am I wearing the Lara Croft clothes?" Erica deadpanned.

"Oh, yeah," Brian answered.

"You couldn't afford me."

Michael and Abby both burst into laughter.

"I could save up my money for a couple of weeks," Brian chuckled, playing along as he slid the dice and book in Erica's direction.

"You still couldn't afford me."

"Months?"

"Maybe a year. Two. Two years." She laughed, and realized that she was feeling almost relaxed. Immediately after that thought came the relief. It was good to just . . . be. She rolled the dice.

"Abby. What is the one thing you've learned about yourself that you wish you knew when you were fifteen?"

"Hello? That I like girls."

"To girls," Brian toasted. They clinked glasses in the middle of the table.

They played on for another half hour before Michael decided to pack it in. "I'm exhausted, my friends. Not to mention a wee bit intoxicated." They all laughed, louder than necessary because they were *all* intoxicated. "I know it's barely seven o'clock, but I slept rather badly last night, as I'm sure we all did, and I'm afraid the jet lag is kicking my sorry behind. Time for me to catch forty winks. Or in this case, about three times that, I hope. It's been fun." He raised his glass in salute, downed the remainder of his drink, and was off.

"And then there were three," Abby said. "Brian."

"What, we're not rolling the dice any more?"

"If you could have prevented any single fashion idea or trend from happening, what would it be?"

"Oh, for god's sake, the damn mullet. Who the hell thought that was a good idea?"

Abby and Erica exchanged glances before both burst into laughter. "Amen to that, my friend," Abby said. "Erica. If you could relive one experience with your mate, what would it be?"

Abby held Erica's gaze and a delicious tension slipped into the room on silent feet, enveloping the two of them. The air seemed to shift and Erica blinked slowly.

"I don't have a mate, so I can't really answer that."

"Me, neither," Brian chimed in, feeling suddenly left out. He raised his glass. "To being single."

"I'll drink to that," Erica said.

"So will I," Abby added, one corner of her mouth turned up in mischief.

They clinked, Abby and Erica never breaking their gaze. Erica snatched the book from Abby's hand, then seemed surprised to have it in her grasp, her vision was that foggy.

"Okay," she said, squinting at a page. "Abby. If you were to be the opposite sex for a single day, what would you do?"

Abby furrowed her dark brows in concentration as if looking for the absolute perfect answer. Brian and Erica waited, watching. "I have two things. Is that okay?"

A nod.

"First, I'd pee standing up." At the ensuing laughter, she went on. "Come on. What woman doesn't wish she could do that?"

"True enough. And then?"

"I'd make love to a woman with my 24-hour dick."

Brian choked on his sip of tequila, recovered, and stood. "And that's my cue." He pretended not to notice how flushed Erica had become. "Ladies, it's been fun. I'll see you tomorrow."

They watched him go and Erica started up from her chair. Abby stopped her with a hand on her forearm.

"Oh, no. I have more questions for you," she said, a glint in her eye.

"I'm drunk." Erica's voice was matter-of-fact.

"I know."

"Aren't you?"

"Yup."

Erica sat.

"Where's the most unusual place you've ever had sex?"

"Sex questions? Is that what we've come to?"

"Apparently," Abby said and cocked an eyebrow expectantly.

"On the dining room table." They both looked at the table in front of them.

"Really?"

"Really."

Abby swallowed. "Have you ever had a threesome?"

"No. Have you?"

"Yes. I don't recommend it. Somebody always ends up feeling left out. What's your favorite part of a woman's body?"

"The place where her neck and shoulder meet." Erica squinted at her suspiciously. "Hey. These aren't 'if' questions."

"They're not?" Abby feigned confusion while sporting a half-grin and turning the book around so she could look at it from various angles.

"You're making these up."

"Could be. What do you wear to bed?"

"Nothing."

Abby swallowed again. Hard. Erica was looking at her, but

obviously not focusing well. They were almost done, Abby knew. "You're fun when you're drunk."

"I know."

"And modest, too."

"I'm just as modest when I'm sober."

"But not as fun." A moment passed. "One last question."

"Okay."

"What the hell's your problem with Walmart?"

Erica burst out laughing, a feminine, musical sound Abby realized she was only hearing for the first time. "You really want to hear my Walmart story? You asked for it."

Abby propped her chin in her hand and listened as Erica spoke.

"I was fourteen," she began as her memory took her back nearly two decades. She wanted to be at the mall. Not because her friends were there—lord knows, she'd had precious few of those. Nobody wanted to be friends with the brainiac—nobody popular anyway. Her closest friend was Julia, and Julia had already gotten her new school clothes. Right there at Walmart. No, Erica wanted to be at the mall so the popular girls would *see* her there, at least *think* they were wrong about where she shopped. That damn Kristy Tarrington could spot a designer knockoff from clear across the classroom and she was never shy about saying so. She'd humiliated Erica on more than one occasion.

Because of that, Erica had given her parents endless amounts of grief about her "cheap, stupid clothes."

"I don't know where you got such expensive taste," her father had said. "When you get a job and you're making your own money, you can buy whatever you want. Until then, you'll get what we can afford or you'll get nothing. Your choice. Understand?"

She'd run to her room in full-out sob mode, screaming that she hated him, teenage oblivion preventing her from comprehending just how much such a remark could hurt. And from that moment on, she'd vowed that once she was employed, she would never, ever buy clothes in a Walmart again. Ever.

Until yesterday.

Abby's face registered new understanding while Erica's flushed pink and she looked away, embarrassed.

"You should take me to bed," she said to Abby.

They looked at each other, Abby with an expression of amused satisfaction until Erica realized what she'd said.

"*Help* me to bed, I mean. *Put* me to bed. Ugh." She covered her eyes with her hand. "I'm going to hate myself in the morning." Removing her hand and glaring, she added, "And you."

"That's a chance I'm willing to take." Abby stood and steadied herself against the table, feeling suddenly more inebriated than she'd thought she was. "Stay here for a second." She gathered the glasses and took them to the kitchen, loaded them into Corinne's dishwasher and set it to run. Back in the dining room, Erica was sitting with her cheek on the table, her arms dangling between her knees. "Ready?" Abby held out a hand. She was startled by how warm and soft Erica's hand was, how snugly it fit into hers.

With some measured maneuvering and deliberate steps, they managed to make it down the basement stairs without becoming a rolling ball of flailing limbs. Once at the bottom, Erica went straight to the bathroom to relieve herself, leaving the door wide open. Abby bit her lip and shook her head, baffled by the enormity of the difference between cool, poised, sober Erica and witty, doesn't-give-a-shit, intoxicated Erica. She stifled a sigh, knowing un-fun Erica would be back in the morning. Probably with a wicked hangover. As Abby wondered how much of tonight's Q & A Erica would remember, Erica came out of the bathroom, removing clothes as she walked.

"Everything okay?" Abby asked as Erica peeled off her T-shirt, then slid off her pants.

"Uh-huh," she responded in bra and panties, both of which were quickly discarded. Abby's eyes widened and she wanted to turn away out of respect, but couldn't bring herself to do so. Erica pulled the covers back and crawled into bed, but not before Abby got an eyeful of milky skin covering flesh that was a glorious combination of curves and muscle. Thick, strong thighs. Rounded, feminine hips. Abby flexed her fingers, clenching her fists to tamp down the desire to run a hand over the roundest, tightest behind she'd ever seen unclothed. Erica flopped onto the mattress on her stomach and pulled the covers over her, nearly jarring Abby out of her trance.

A deep breath in and then out slowly, Abby wet her lips and pulled herself together. In the bathroom, she found some Motrin and a glass, which she filled with water. Catching Erica before she passed out, Abby ordered her, "Here. Take these and drink this water. You'll thank me in the morning."

Forty-five minutes later, Erica was snoring like a truck driver and Abby was still awake. She lay on the loveseat with her feet propped up on the arm and hanging over, not exactly comfortable, but she'd slept on worse. It was barely nine-thirty and she was exhausted, but she couldn't get her mind to turn off. It went from the horrifying visions of the towers collapsing and people plummeting to their deaths, to the smiling faces of Tim and Corinne MacDougal, to Michael and Brian clacking their shot glasses together, to Erica's pale, beautiful body crawling naked into bed. Around and around the pictures went until Abby thought she'd go insane. The next time the towers appeared in her mind's eye, she got up and quietly rummaged until she found Erica's cell phone, reminding herself once again that she really should get one of her own. She left the bathroom light on, then took the phone outside and dialed. When there was no answer at home, she took a chance and dialed her mother's office number at the museum. Luck was with her.

"Mom?" Hearing her mother's voice was such a relief, it brought tears to Abby's eyes.

"Abby, baby, how are you? Are you still in Canada?" Michelle Hayes sounded tired. She sounded surprised, thankful, and happy to hear her daughter's voice, but mostly, she sounded exhausted.

"I'm okay. How are you? You're still at work?"

"Oh, Abby. It's all so awful. It's just . . . it's crazy here. It's nuts. People don't know what to do. Traffic is a disaster. Hundreds are missing. It's just . . . it's awful. I'm actually glad you're not here right now. Are you okay there? Is it terrible?"

"I'm fine, Mom. Don't worry." She relayed the story of the MacDougals and what they'd done for their little foursome. It soon became obvious that her stories were helping to calm Michelle, so she continued, telling about the Walmart trip, about dinner, about the game. By the time she finished, her mother was almost chuckling, the smile apparent in her voice.

"Any idea when you'll be here?"

"You probably have a better handle on that than I do," Abby told her. "We haven't heard anything; it's kind of remote here. I do know that nearly forty planes landed here, so there have to be thousands of people stranded like me and nobody's allowed to get their baggage."

"You're safe. That's all that matters right now, believe me. I'm so thankful I'm not one of those poor people wandering the streets outside trying to find their loved ones. I can't imagine."

"You're safe, too. Right?"

"I'm fine, baby. I decided to stay here for the night simply because it's too crazy to go out there. The subway is packed, cabs are at a standstill."

"Sounds like staying put is smart."

"There are seven of us here. I have a change of clothes in my gym bag and one of the higher-ups has a shower he's letting us use. There's a cafeteria downstairs, so we have food. We're fine. It just makes more sense."

"Good."

They spoke a little longer about mundane things, mostly just to keep hearing each other's voice. Abby was reluctant to hang up, but worried about the cell phone bill she could be causing. And the irritation Erica would have when she found out. Abby briefly wondered if she could keep Erica drunk for the remainder of their stay.

Back in the basement, Erica hadn't moved and still sounded like a chain saw, which brought a smile to Abby's face. The cat had reappeared and was curled up between Erica's legs.

"Lucky cat," Abby muttered as she put the phone back where she'd found it. The bathroom light made it easy for her to see, and she paused to study Erica's face. The same thing she'd noticed at the Lions Club struck her again: how relaxed Erica looked while asleep and what a departure it was from her usual stern, studied gaze. Her face was relaxed, the skin smooth, all the scowl lines and worry creases gone and nothing left but a creamy, even complexion sprinkled with freckles. A corkscrew of auburn hair fell over one closed eye, and Abby gently moved it. As she did so, she wondered for the umpteenth time just what it was that kept Erica from being more comfortable in her own skin, why she was so serious, so contemplative, so reserved. Alcohol had loosened her up and loosened her up quickly. Abby found that interesting. She wondered if that meant the grave and stoic exterior was just that: an exterior. If maybe the fun, witty Erica she'd seen tonight was actually the *real* Erica, the one who was being hidden. But why?

And why did she care? That was the biggest question of all. Why should Abby give a shit? After all, they were going to go their separate ways eventually, probably sooner rather than later, and she would probably never cross Erica's mind again. So why should she expend so much time and energy on trying to figure out a woman she'd most likely never see again after this ordeal?

That was the question that stayed with her as she re-settled herself on the loveseat, adjusted blankets, punched and reshaped pillows, and attempted to get at least a few hours of sleep. It stayed with her because she had no answer.

September 13, 2001
Thursday

Chapter 8

"Wow! Erica? Erica Ryan? Is that really you? You look . . . fabulous."
The expression on Kristy Tarrington's shockingly pudgy face said the words forced their way past her lips, that she wanted to say anything but them.
"Yes. Yes, it's me. Erica Ryan. Graduate of the same high school as you." Erica was on a stage, under a spotlight, and wearing a to-die-for emerald green bikini. Kristy was right: she looked fabulous. Striking a model's pose, she tucked a hand on her hip and stood with one foot slightly in front of the other as she spoke. "The same girl you called an ugly nerd, a hopeless wannabe, and . . . what was the other one? Oh, yeah. A sad and pathetic specimen of the human female. Wasn't that it?"
Kristy grimaced, giving prominence to all three of her chins. "Oh, come on. We were kids. That stuff didn't mean anything."
Erica's eyes flew open wide. "Didn't mean anything? To who? To you? I've got news for you, Kristy. It sure meant something to me. You ruined my teenage years. You made me feel like crap, day in and day out. The things you said to me all through high school, the names you called me—they shaped how I think about myself even today. I'm thirty-two years old, for god's sake, and I can still remember how worthless you made me feel. Don't you get that?"
Kristy shrugged. "Jesus, Erica. Don't you think it's time you get over that stuff? I mean, really, it's been more than ten years."
Erica was appalled. Was it supposed to go this way? Wasn't Kristy supposed to apologize? She blinked rapidly, searching for something to say, horrified that she felt small, insignificant, and sixteen all over again.
"You got fat." It was the best she could come up with.
"Yup," Kristy replied, pulling a cheeseburger out of thin air. She took a bite and looked above Erica's head as she chewed. "Heads up."

71

Erica followed her gaze just in time to see the light grid falling down on top of her, smashing into her skull, causing immediate and splintering pain . . .

Pain.

Throbbing.

Pain and throbbing. The only things of which she was aware.

Throbbing like timpani being beaten inside her head and pain like jackhammers pounding against the interior of her skull.

"Ugh."

She was afraid to move. She was afraid to open her eyes. A mental inventory told her that she was in bed on her stomach. Her right arm was under the pillow beneath her head and had fallen asleep some time ago; she couldn't feel it. Her mouth felt pasty, her tongue stuck to the roof of her mouth and her teeth sporting furry little sweaters. Her legs were splayed in opposite directions, a strange vibration humming against her left calf.

And she was completely naked.

"Morning, sunshine."

The voice was so close to her ear, Erica started as if she'd been poked in the ribs. "Jesus Christ."

"Oh, honey, I don't think he can help you today."

Abby. Damn her, she was enjoying this. Erica could hear the amusement in her tone. "What the hell did you do to me?" Her voice barely sounded like her own, more like gravel in a blender. She tried to clear her throat without moving her head or opening her eyes.

"It wasn't me. I tried to help. I gave you water and Motrin before you passed out. How's the head?"

"Feels like it's been rolling around in a dryer."

"Yeah, tequila will do that to you."

"Ugh. I hate tequila."

"Didn't look that way last night."

Erica groaned.

"Do you want me to see what Corinne's got to eat?"

"God, no." Erica's stomach churned a warning at the mere thought of food.

"I didn't think so. You should drink some water, though. You're dehydrated."

Finally, finally, Erica cracked one eye open and focused on her temporary roomie. She looked fresh as a newly blossomed flower, smelling of baby powder, the ends of her dark hair still damp and leaving wet spots on her T-shirt. "Why aren't you like this?" she muttered in annoyance.

"I am one of the few people tequila is actually nice to," Abby explained, so cheerfully that Erica wanted to bust her in the mouth. If only she could lift her right arm. "I was a little tipsy last night, but . . ." Abby trailed off, arching an eyebrow.

"Not like me."

"No. Not like you."

"How did I end up nude?" Covering her face, Erica pleaded, "Tell me you didn't have to help me."

"I didn't have to help you. You got undressed all by yourself."

Visible through her fingers, the trail of clothes from the bathroom to the bed told her all she needed to know. "Oh, god. You were here, weren't you?"

"Yes. I kept you from coming down the stairs on your face."

"And I undressed right in front of you?"

"Oh, yes."

"Oh, god." Erica pulled the covers over her head. From under them, she shouted, "And stop enjoying this so much!"

Abby laughed, but it was kind, not teasing, not at her expense. Erica peeked out, made a face. "I'm so embarrassed."

"Believe me, Erica, you have no reason to be." She waggled her eyebrows lasciviously and Erica took a halfhearted swipe at her. "I'm going to go grab some breakfast and bring you down some juice or something, okay? Just lie here, take your time. There's no hurry. I don't think we're getting out of here today."

Though it wasn't the news Erica wanted to hear, not having to force herself to get up was a relief. Besides, she didn't know if a herd of elephants stampeding through the room right now would get her to move. Her limbs felt filled with concrete and her head was too foggy for any attempt at raising it.

73

"Okay," she agreed. "I'll be right here if you need me."

Abby patted her shoulder and headed upstairs.

"Ugh," Erica said aloud, again, just to say something. She tried hard to focus her brain, to make herself remember the previous night. She was worried she'd done something worse than strip in front of a virtual stranger, concerned she'd said something stupid. Or worse, provocative. Alcohol usually made her kind of flirty, but last night, all she could remember was sober, then trashed—and nothing in between. She'd have to ask Abby later and hope she'd be honest.

Abby.

What was it about her? There was something Erica couldn't put a finger on, something that intrigued her—which was unusual because Erica rarely bothered with people. People were unreliable, fallible, needy, and they made her uncomfortable. Her boss was unendingly telling her what an asset she was to the science lab because she didn't get caught up in personal stuff: she was all about the facts, the organization, the marketing. He liked that; he wanted that running his lab.

Abby, though; Abby interested her, much as she hated to admit it. She also annoyed her and irritated her and rubbed her the wrong way. But she was interesting just the same. She didn't make her cringe as much as she had that first time in the airport, and Erica wondered why. Was Pollyanna actually growing on her? Did Pollyanna actually *like* her? No, that couldn't be.

Most people found Erica cold. She knew that, and she tried not to let it bother her. Shrugging it off had always been her response. That's how she'd managed to get through high school, and it was a method she carried on into adulthood. She'd taught herself not to care. And it had worked very well until recently, the past year or two. Maddie—the one who'd given her the Cartier watch for their one-year anniversary—had snapped that an iceberg had more warmth than Erica. The next day, she packed up and left for good, leaving Erica to wonder for the first time since the ninth grade exactly what kind of person she'd allowed herself to become. She hadn't liked the answers and so she'd spent the next year-and-a-half trying to avoid them, submerging herself in her work and unwittingly isolating herself, walling herself off. Erica wasn't a stupid woman, not by any stretch of the imagination. Somewhere deep inside, she knew such segregation was unhealthy, but she continued on that same course for months until her life outside of work consisted mostly of, well, her.

And now here she was, in Gander, Newfoundland, stranded in a house full of people, naked and hungover in the bed of a total stranger.

What the fuck?

ᏍᏇ ᏍᏈ ᏍᏇ

Brian followed his nose down the stairs and into the kitchen, the scent of freshly brewed coffee the only thing driving him. His head throbbed, though not quite as badly as he'd expected. It was probably a good thing he'd bowed out of last night's shenanigans when he had. A couple more shots and he'd have spent much of the night praying to the porcelain god. Luckily, he'd simply passed out and slept straight through the night. He woke up disoriented and alarmingly thirsty, but no worse for wear.

Abby was humming quietly in the kitchen as she poured two mugs of coffee, looking as if she hadn't had anything to drink the night before, let alone just as much as the rest of them. Well, him and Erica anyway.

"He's out for a run?" Brian said with thinly veiled disgust as he read the note on the counter.

"Michael was the smartest one of all of us last night."

"I hate him."

Abby nodded with a quiet laugh.

"Is one of those for me?" Brian gestured to the mugs with his chin.

"Um, yes. As a matter of fact." She pulled another mug from the cupboard, handed a full one to Brian, and filled the third.

"So, three of us are accounted for. Where's the fourth?"

"Still in bed."

"Crying?"

Abby barked a laugh. "Maybe. She's a hurtin' unit, that's for sure. I don't think an evening of shots is a regular occurrence for her."

"I don't think it's a regular occurrence for any of us. But for her especially. In fact, I don't think an evening of people is a regular occurrence for her." He took a sip of his coffee and dipped his head appreciatively. Hot, black, and strong, just the way he liked it.

"You got that impression, too?"

"Oh, yeah. She seemed to loosen up, though."

"I thought she was fun."

"She was. And I think she actually strung more than two sentences together at one time."

"I think she's just shy," Abby said, a hint of defensiveness in her voice.

"Or an uptight bitch." At Abby's gasp, he grinned. "I'm kidding. Well, not about the uptight part. I don't know her well enough to know if she's a bitch."

"You're terrible."

"She's hot, though. What an ass on her." Brian sucked air in through his teeth.

"You have no idea."

"You tap that?"

"What? No! But . . ." She let her voice trail off, a mischievous glint in her eye.

Brian glanced at the closed basement door and lowered his voice, took a step toward Abby. "What? You saw something, didn't you? Tell me!"

"I can't. It's disrespectful."

Brian scoffed. "Oh, please. You were being far from respectful with the questions you were asking last night. No, you don't get to fall back on respect." At her look of hesitation, he decided to resort to begging. "Please, Abby. I'm divorced. I'm only in my thirties. Do you think celibacy does it for a guy like me? Come on, throw me a bone. Pun intended. Give me some material."

Abby hesitated. But one look at Brian's face, at the hangdog expression and she thought, *That's what she gets for stripping in front of me like that.* She relayed the whole story to Brian.

"God." Brian dropped into a chair as if his legs gave out. "My god."

"Guys are so easy," Abby said with a good-natured eye-roll.

"And you really didn't hit that?"

She cocked her head. "And that, my friend, is the difference between men and women. Call me crazy, but sleeping with an intoxicated, half-unconscious woman is not my idea of a good time."

Brian narrowed his eyes. "Tell me you didn't think about it."

"Bri." Abby leveled a gaze at him. "She was trashed."

His shoulders slumped and he blew out a breath. "Man, I hate my ex-wife. This divorce has turned me into a sex-crazed pig."

"Eh." Abby waved him off dismissively. "You're a guy. You didn't have that far to go."

He laughed. "Hey, did you see Tim or Corinne this morning?"

"Yup. Tim headed off to work and dropped Corinne at the Lions Club, so they could leave us these." She dangled a set of keys in front of him.

His eyes widened in disbelief. "Are those car keys?"

"That they are."

"They left us a car?"

"That they did."

"What is wrong with them?"

Abby shrugged. "They're Canadian."

ଔ ଔ ଔ

They puttered for a few hours, letting Erica ease into the day and waiting for Michael to return from his run and then shower. By noon, Erica had swallowed (and kept down) a slice of dry toast and two cups of coffee, and all four of them were ready for a change of scenery, so they decided to go for a ride. Abby was elected to drive. Michael took shotgun while Brian and Erica piled into the back seat.

It was another unseasonably warm day (or so the car radio reported) and Gander was beautiful. Lush and green, lusher than the flat, rural area where Erica had grown up, greener than the urban brick and mortar Abby knew.

The town wasn't big, so finding the main routes took only a little bit of driving, and Tim had left a map to make it that much easier. People were milling everywhere, up and down streets, hanging out in front of buildings, wandering aimlessly like zombies in a bad sci-fi movie. They were trying to pass the time as they hung in limbo, waiting for the moment they'd be told they could board their planes again, that they could resume their lives.

"Hey, look at that," Michael said, pointing to their left. Outside a building marked Newtel Communications, long tables were set up under outdoor tents. Some held telephones, others held computers. Hand-lettered signs boasted no-charge phone calls and internet access. "All free. Amazing."

"Corinne said the pharmacy is filling prescriptions for free, too," Abby said.

Brian's voice was low, in awe. "These people are really something."

"What's this highlighted part?" Michael asked, pointing at bright yellow on the map.

"Turn it around," Abby said, making a spinning motion with a finger. "See the gander head?"

"Well, I'll be damned."

She was right. Three streets: Elizabeth, Edinburgh, and Memorial, all curved and met in such a way as to form a crude outline of the head of a goose.

"That's where the town got its name. Tim told me."

"Huh. Clever."

"I was thinking maybe we could go to Cobb's Pond." She glanced at the map and pointed in the general vicinity. "Tim said there's a boardwalk and it's such a nice day. You all up for a stroll?"

Fifteen minutes later, Abby and Erica were waving goodbye to the men in the car, who promised they'd be back in two hours or less.

"Is walking along a boardwalk a girly thing or something?" Abby asked, a little stung that the guys didn't hang around.

"Yeah, it kind of is," Erica replied, amused by Abby's pout.

"Too bad for them," Abby declared with a shrug. "Look at this place. It's gorgeous."

She was right about that. A large archway announced Cobb's Pond Rotary Park and beyond it, beautiful blue water and the deep, thick green of fir, birch, aspen, and spruce trees. Other people milled about, dining at various picnic tables or launching canoes for a relaxing glide around the pond, but overall the atmosphere was quiet and peaceful. Erica sucked in a big lungful of air and let it out slowly.

"Feeling better?" Abby asked, noting that the blue of Erica's eyes had brightened since earlier that morning.

"Much." She turned to look at Abby. "Thank you."

"No problem." Abby pointed. "Hey, that looks like the board-walk. Tim said it goes all the way around, between three and four kilometers." She laughed. "And I have no idea how far that is."

"A little over two miles."

"Figures you'd know that. You up for it?"

With a quick dip of her head, Erica headed for the boardwalk, Abby jogged to catch up.

They spent nearly fifteen minutes walking in silence, simply enjoying their surroundings. Birds were plentiful, as were squirrels, both feeding from the various feeders and houses scattered throughout the trees. Observation decks were spaced every so often for stopping and looking out over the pond, and breathing in the beauty of it all—the water, the birdsong, the clean air. Erica could feel her body relaxing, finally; the first time she'd been able to let go in several days. Her shoulders seemed to soften, the rock hardness of that area finally melting away. Her lungs felt clear, like every last molecule of airplane air was finally, only now, gone from her system. Muscles that had felt taut as stretched rubber bands gradually relaxed, the rigidity easing, and her pale skin soaked in the rays of the sun. She turned her face toward the sky, eyes closed, content.

No wonder the people of Gander were so wonderful, she thought. How could you not be happy here?

It was the most foreign feeling she'd had in ages. And it was so amazing it nearly brought tears to her eyes.

Abby was in tune with people, a characteristic on which she prided herself, and she watched the change come over Erica with interest. She saw it happening, saw her relax, saw the worry lines on her face smooth out, saw the almost-smile that turned up the corners of her mouth. It was quite a sight. She wanted to ask if Erica was all right, but didn't want to send her skittering back into her shell. Instead, they walked a bit farther in silence. When it felt right, Abby spoke.

"It's beautiful here."

"It really is."

"Where I grew up in Connecticut, it's very green and there are lots of trees like this, but I was never close to a lake or anything. Were you?"

"No. It's pretty flat and dry where I grew up."

"What about where you live now? In Raleigh, you said?"

Erica pursed her lovely lips, thinking. "It's gorgeous there. Very green, lots of trees and lakes and trails for walking or biking." The pursed lips changed into a slight frown. "I don't get to enjoy it as much as I'd like."

"Work?" When Erica nodded, she asked, "What do you do?"

"I'm a research scientist at a pharmaceutical company and I manage a team of other scientists."

"Cool." Abby was impressed.

"It can be."

"But?"

"But my seven-hundred-dollar bicycle has become a clothes rack in my apartment," Erica replied.

"I see. Too much work and not enough play make Erica a dull girl."

"You don't know the half of it."

"So why were you in the U.K.?"

"I was meeting with a division of our company, trying to pitch

80

a new drug, which turned out to be a disaster." She blew out a breath and watched a hawk soar high above the trees. "Enough about me. What about you?"

"What about me?"

"What do you do?"

"I'm sort of between jobs right now."

Erica squinted at her. "Between jobs?"

"Yeah. I was a business major and I had a job in a small, up-and-coming company near home, but . . ." Her voice trailed off as she glanced over the water to their left.

"But?"

"I hated it."

"What did you hate about it?"

Abby sighed, floundered around for the right words. "I just felt used up at the end of the day, you know? I was working ten-, sometimes twelve-hour days. I was exhausted. I never saw my family—and I was still living in my mother's house. I was making good money but I didn't have time to spend any of it. After a year-and-a-half, I decided I just couldn't do it any more. I quit."

"Wow." Quitting was something Erica had never done, not in her entire life. It was something she frowned upon, something her father frowned upon even more. Abby's reasons made sense, but still. Erica had a tough time seeing herself doing the same thing. "You just decided one day you'd had enough and you just left?"

"Exactly. I believe in happiness, you know? I believe we all have the right to live our lives as happy people. If we all did that, the world would be a better place, that's for sure."

"You're probably right about that," Erica agreed, trying hard to imagine what it would be like to just up and quit her job, just walk out one day. "Did you have something else lined up before you left?"

"Nope."

"No?"

Abby shook her head, amused by Erica's shock.

"So, you just left. With nothing to head to? No plan?"

"Didn't need one."

"Wow," Erica said again, wondering how incredibly irresponsible she'd have to be to do such a thing, especially living with her parents. Her father would kill her. "What did your parents say?"

"They got it, you know? They totally understood and supported me. They're awesome."

"They didn't push you to find another job?"

"Nah. I mean, I'm sure they wanted me to. Want me to. But, they know I will. When it's right."

When it's right? Erica had no idea what to say. The delicious relaxation of a few minutes ago was draining away like water through her fingers. Her brain kept tossing her images of her father's reddened and angry face as he tried to wrap his brain around the fact that his daughter was a quitter with no plan for her future. He wanted her to be happy, sure; he wasn't an ogre. But he also expected her to work hard, even when she didn't want to, just as he had. It was the way he was raised, the way he and her mother had raised her. Work hard, pull your weight, be responsible. Abby's choices just didn't compute.

Abby was still talking, looking dreamily at the sky. "I don't want to spend my entire life doing something I hate. And I want to give back, you know?"

"Give back?"

"Yeah, like volunteer. Help the less fortunate. Plant trees. Take care of the animals." She scoffed. "Too bad that stuff doesn't pay better, huh?"

"Right." Erica had never volunteered for anything in her life; she was too busy working. She'd had a steady job since she'd turned fifteen and started working at her father's feed store (so she didn't have to get her wardrobe from Walmart). From then on, she'd always, *always* pulled her own weight, never expected anybody to carry her. She'd not be able to bear it if she still lived at home. The shame of burdening her parents would be too much for her. She'd die of humiliation. She snuck a glance at Abby, who was smiling widely, obviously satisfied by her decisions in life. Erica was uncertain whether she admired the woman, envied her, or was disgusted by her. "So, what do you do while you're between jobs? Why were you in England?"

"I've been traveling like crazy. I love it. I've been trying to see as much of the world as possible."

"And how do you pay for all this traveling?" It was a rude question, but it popped out of Erica's mouth before she could stop it. Besides, she really wanted to know.

Abby chuckled, but Erica thought it contained a sliver of uncertainty. "I told you, I was making good money when I was working. I was living at home, so I was able to save some up. Plus, I'm good at traveling cheaply."

"I see."

This time, Abby's laugh was a bark, a quick staccato burst that startled Erica. "No, you don't."

"What?"

"You don't see at all. You've been silently judging me this whole time. Do you think I can't tell?" She wasn't angry, and she could see right through Erica.

"I'm not sure what you mean."

"You think I'm lazy."

Erica's head snapped around and she caught her eye. "What? No. I never said that."

"But you don't agree with my decisions."

"Your decisions are your decisions."

"But you don't agree with them."

"It doesn't matter what *I* think."

"I'm asking you what you think."

Erica stopped walking and they stood facing each other. "Why?"

"Because I'm interested in your opinion."

"Why?" Erica asked again.

"Why not?" Abby shrugged, her expression playful.

"You don't even know me."

"True. So what's the big deal about giving your opinion to a stranger?"

Abby's lighthearted tone was starting to grate on Erica and

she suspected that Abby knew it. She tried to keep from taking the bait, but Abby was determined.

"Don't you ever take anything seriously?" Erica said. "Is everything a game to you?"

"Is that what you think?" Again, no anger, no hurt in Abby's voice, just curiosity. "That I'm a perpetual clown?"

"That nothing is a big deal to you? Yeah. You do come across that way." She tried to soften her words. "A little bit." She began walking again, Abby falling in step next to her.

"I just like to have fun," Abby said. "I don't think there's anything wrong with that. Like I said, if more people would focus on being happy rather than on being rich, the world would be a much better place."

"Maybe." Erica's tone said she doubted it.

"Come on. Haven't you ever just, I don't know, cut loose? Thrown caution to the wind? Lived in the moment?"

They held each other's gaze, then both spoke at the same time.

"No, huh?"

"Not really, no."

A moment passed and then suddenly they were laughing. Laughing at the silly circular path of their conversation. Laughing at being trapped in another country. Laughing at their impromptu outfits. Laughing at whatever they could laugh at to keep their minds off the situation back in the States, to keep from thinking about the thousands of people crushed to death in the towers, to keep from thinking about the grief of those who were endlessly, achingly searching for their missing loved ones, to keep from thinking about how badly they wanted to go home.

Chapter 9

She should be exhausted. After the Night of Poor Judgment (as she was now referring to her foray into the Land of Tequila, where she hoped to never visit again, and the hour-long walk around the pond, Erica thought she'd be ready for a nap. Instead, she felt a weird sense of energy, like she'd tapped some area of reserve in her body that revved her up, made her hum like a machine.

Alone in the basement, she reveled in the quiet. The four of them—Erica, Abby, Brian, and Michael—had lunch together at a little diner, which was filled to capacity with Plane People (as the locals had taken to calling them). After that, Abby had wanted to drop by the Lions Club and check on the Bakers, see how Corinne was doing, visit the couple with the new baby, be social—which was fine, but Erica opted out. The situation alone overloaded her brain. She knew she should probably tag along, but she wasn't good at small talk, never had been. She was sure she'd only end up feeling awkward, thereby making others feel awkward, and that was the last thing anybody needed. So she asked to be dropped off, claiming a headache. None of the other three argued with that.

The basement was cool and comfortable. She knew she was free to be upstairs, to watch TV or help herself to the kitchen, but she felt intrusive. Corinne and Tim had been beyond kind, beyond generous, and Erica was certain they wouldn't be fazed in the least to find her on their couch watching some daytime talk show or soap. Hell, they'd probably be happy about it, but she didn't feel right doing so. The basement was easier, felt safer, more allowed. She dropped onto the foot of the bed, leaned back on her hands, and blew out a breath as she kicked her sneakered feet. For the first time, Erica was glad she'd followed Abby's advice and purchased these sporty clothes. Thinking ahead, Erica had purchased two similar sets in different colors, uncertain as to how long she'd be stranded. She knew a washer and dryer stood behind the closed doors in the corner and she wondered if Corinne would let her toss a load in later that night. At this point, who knew how long it would be before they were able to go home? For all she knew, she could be here for weeks.

Stress seized her at the thought and she quickly tried to focus on something else. The cat appeared, seemingly out of nowhere, and curled up next to her thigh.

Kate MacDougal was a reader. There must have been a hundred books stacked on the shelves every which way. Erica imagined they had been neat at one time, lined up next to each other, maybe even alphabetically. But as more books arrived and were read, Kate had to fit them in where she could: on top of the rows, in stacks on the very tops of the shelves, piled on the floor. The range of authors was wide, from classics like Jane Austen and Virginia Woolf to biographies of Ingrid Bergman and Arthur Ashe to bestsellers from Dean Koontz and Nora Roberts. Her tastes were all over the map, kind of like Abby.

She flopped back onto the bed and stared at the acoustic tile of the ceiling while she scratched absently at the purring feline (what the hell was his name anyway?) and recalled their earlier conversation. She'd been so appalled over the idea of quitting a job with no notice and sponging off parents that she didn't really give herself any time to roll it around in her head, examine it from different angles. That was how she usually approached things that she had trouble reconciling and it made her good at her job. She didn't want to admit to the fact that Abby was actually growing on her, considering how determined she'd been to dislike her on sight. But because Erica almost liked the woman, she found herself wanting to analyze the decisions Abby had made. If she was going to be honest, Erica had to confess there was something almost admirable about quitting a job simply because you were unhappy.

Again, she thought of her father, but this time instead of stressing out over the image, she almost laughed. Jim Ryan would absolutely blow a gasket if she told him she'd left her job and was moving in with him until she felt the "time was right" to find new employment, but this time the thought of his face reddening like a beet, his mouth opening and closing like a fish's as he searched for the right words to express his disapproval, was nearly cartoonish.

"Good thing I don't hate my job," she said aloud to the empty space around her. Not that there weren't things she'd change about it. She worked way too many hours, the ratio of time she spent at work versus the time she spent at home alarmingly unbalanced. She liked her coworkers. They respected her and she them, but she often felt something was missing. She just didn't know what it was.

Her brain drifted from topic to topic as she lay there alone with the cat, his purring the only sound in the house. What were other Plane People doing today? Did any of them have a clue about when they'd be allowed to go home? She'd heard some people at the table behind her at lunch in the diner talking about a shopkeeper offering her shower to them, so she knew the MacDougals weren't the only people in Gander vying for sainthood. And another woman walked by them conversing with her companion, confirming Abby's statement that the pharmacy was filling prescriptions for free. For the umpteenth time, Erica wondered just what was in the water in Gander that made everybody so kind and generous. It was bizarre and she doubted such selflessness would be shown in America.

With a squirm and a shift, she rolled onto her side so she was spooning the cat, boredom and excess energy warring within her body. Abby's backpack sat in a corner against the bookshelves and brought Erica's mind back to the subject of her . . . what? Roommate? Fellow Plane Person? New friend? From her vantage point in back of the passenger seat of the

MacDougals' car, Erica'd had ample opportunity to study Abby without her knowledge. She'd tried to avoid it, but Abby's laugh kept pulling Erica's eyes back toward her. She wore her dark hair in a ponytail again today, and it corkscrewed along the back of her neck. Erica's gaze had stuck there for what felt like a long time, focused on the smooth skin, the short, probably soft hairs that rebelled against the rubber band, the curve of muscle and sinew where Abby's neck met her shoulder. Erica didn't know anybody who had 'smiling' eyes, but Abby did. The blue of them was the color of the summer sky, and small crinkles in the corners were a testament to how often she grinned or laughed. She was perpetually cheerful, even in this trying situation.

"I don't know how she does it," Erica stated to the cat, who regarded her silently. "Do you?"

The cat looked at her with its cat eyes—eyes that seemed too green to be real—and yawned widely.

"Nice."

Finding her mind drifting back yet again to Abby—this time to the hard muscles of her calves as well as the deceptively long legs—Erica sat up with a frustrated groan, annoyed with herself.

"What the hell is wrong with me?" she asked the cat. "I just have some excess energy, right? No big deal. Lots of people have excess energy. It's nothing to stress about. I just need to channel it in another direction. Before I go crazy. Or my head explodes. That's all." She scanned the room and her eyes fell on the treadmill. "See? Perfect."

Exercise was exactly what she needed to release some of her pent-up energy. At home, work usually didn't allow time for her to feel restless and jumpy. She was always busy, always focused on the next project or the current project or both. Being stuck in one place without much to do was very new to her. Not only did she not like the feeling, she also worried she wasn't handling it well. Running a couple of miles would surely help clear her mind.

Wishing she had her own Sauconys from home, she hoped the sneakers she'd bought would suffice. She pulled her hair back off her face, tightened her laces, and perused the control panel of Kate MacDougal's treadmill.

CR CB CR

Several blocks away, Brian and Michael saw Tim in the parking lot of the Lions Club unloading some supplies and offered their assistance. Abby went inside, looking for the Bakers. The Lions club was abuzz with activity, noise from the Plane People—telephone conversations, children playing, babies crying—interspersed with noise from the locals—delivering supplies, cleaning up used items, directing people toward stores, churches, and parks. Both televisions still stood in the corner, reporting the latest on the situation in the States. Abby had avoided the news at all costs, but felt the sudden desire to check in with her mother again. All the phones were occupied, but she kept an eye on them as she scanned the area.

Abby was bummed that Erica had chosen to stay at the house, having realized during their walk that she was growing to like Erica, despite the differences in their personalities. They didn't have a ton in common, but Abby found her interesting to talk to, fun to tease, and fascinating to look at. She wished her new friend was still with her. Their walk around Cobb's Pond had been wonderful—relaxing, stimulating, and enlightening. Erica certainly wasn't the first person over thirty who'd tried to hide disapproval over her current state of unemployment and how she'd gotten there, but it didn't matter to Abby. She was perfectly comfortable in her decisions and as long as she knew she had her parents' support, whatever anybody else thought didn't matter to her. It was a freeing attitude because it allowed her to defend and debate her stance without getting angry or too personally entrenched. Rather than becoming insulted, she'd actually enjoyed the little bit of sparring with Erica. It got her blood pumping.

Across the lobby area, exiting the ladies' room was Mrs. Baker. Abby barely recognized her. Was it possible for somebody to age ten years in only two days? The poor woman had enormous bags under her eyes, the circles dark and plainly visible. Her cocoa brown eyes drooped with sadness and worry, and she wrung her hands habitually. Abby's heart cracked a little at the sight.

"Hey, you," she said as she approached, wrapping her arms around Mrs. Baker's shoulders. "How're you holding up? Any news?"

Mrs. Baker leaned into her. "Nothing yet. My daughter is calling here every couple of hours, trying to keep us informed, but nobody's heard from him yet. That can't be good."

"Don't give up." Abby faltered, wondering what on earth she could possibly say that would make any of it any better. "Tyson needs you to stay strong right now. Don't give up. Okay?"

"Okay." Mrs. Baker squeezed her. "How'd you get to be such a shining star, huh? I'll say it again: your mama raised you right."

"Yes, she did. How's the old man? Is he hanging in there?"

Mrs. Baker gestured toward the TV corner with her chin. "He's been over there watching those news reports for hours. I don't know what he hopes to learn. I can't do it. I just can't watch all that pain and destruction. Not while my boy might be in the thick of it, you know?"

Abby nodded, absently wondering if Mr. Baker hoped to get a glimpse of his son running in front of the camera as he emerged from the rubble. Everybody handled stress in their own way. She wondered what she'd do in the Bakers' situation. What would Erica do, for that matter? Brian? Michael? Corinne? Most likely, everybody would do something different.

She walked Mrs. Baker back to her cot, keeping an arm around her the whole time. "What can I do? Do you need anything?"

Mrs. Baker sat down with the heaving sigh of an exhausted person. "Would you be a dear and see if my husband wants anything to eat or drink? He hasn't had anything since coffee this morning and he really needs to eat, but—" She swallowed and a wave of shame crossed her face. "I don't think I can bear being around those news reports. They give me too many horrible things to imagine, you understand what I'm saying?"

"Absolutely." Abby squeezed her shoulder. "I'll take care of it."

She studied Mr. Baker as she approached him. He had the same worried, worn-out appearance as his wife. His clothes were wrinkled along with his face, and the expectation of bad news was as clear as day in his deep-set brown eyes. "Hey, handsome," she said when she got to him.

He looked up at her, blinked three times until he registered the face. "Abby. Hey there." He looked pleased to see her as he held out his enormous hand and engulfed her smaller one. "Sit. How've you been? I heard you were sprung from this place."

She grinned. "I was. Corinne said she asked you and the Mrs. before the guys that ended up coming with us."

"Such a sweet woman, that one."

"She sure is."

"She did offer us her home." He swallowed and spared a glance in his wife's direction. "Tonya didn't want to be away from the phones, since this is the number our daughter has. I tried to tell her we could just give her a different number, but my wife likes to stay put in a crisis. I think it helps calm her down a little bit."

Abby nodded, wishing there was something she could say to ease his heartbreak.

"Can you believe this shit?" he asked her, waving a finger at the television. "How does this happen? Four different planes. How the hell does this happen?"

Abby shook her head as her eyes were pulled unwillingly towards the screen. Live shots ran nonstop, the spot where the twin towers once stood now just a pile of concrete and debris. Though the scene was calmer than two days ago, there were still people milling around behind the reporter, looking lost and wandering aimlessly. Some cried. Some looked blank. Flyers with photos of the missing had begun to appear in the background of every shot—covering fences, telephone poles, and the sides of buildings like wallpaper. The whole thing was still surreal to Abby. "I don't know," she finally said in response to Mr. Baker's question. "I just don't know."

They watched together for a few quiet moments, neither registering that he still held tightly to Abby's hand. She was happy to give him that contact, even if it helped only a little. When a commercial break finally came, she squeezed his big fingers. "Hey, a little birdie told me you haven't eaten anything today. Am I going to have to spank you?" She winked and got a small chortle out of him.

"I'm just not hungry."

"I'm sure you're not. I get it. But you should try to eat something anyway to help keep up your strength. Even if it's just a banana or an apple."

"I know."

"I'll go find you something, all right? Wait here."

"I'm not going anywhere," he said as she stood. "Unfortunately."

After delivering a banana, a granola bar, and some orange juice to Mr. Baker, waiting for him to eat some, and tossing a thumbs up toward his wife, Abby took the opportunity to snag an empty seat at the phone bank and call her mother. This time, she tried the office phone first. Michelle Hayes picked up on the second ring.

"Is everything okay?" The worry in her voice was apparent, given she'd just spoken to Abby the previous night.

"Everything's fine, Mom. I just—" It came upon her without warning. Emotion. Sadness. Anger. Her voice stuck in her throat and she said in a whisper, "I just wanted to hear your voice. I *needed* to hear your voice."

"Oh, baby. My sweet baby." Michelle knew her daughter well, knew when something was weighing on her, and wanted nothing more than to wrap her up in a warm, safe hug. "It's going to be okay, Abby."

"I know." Abby sniffed, pulled herself together, embarrassed to be seen crying. She swiped at her eyes. "It's just so horrible. There are people here who can't get a hold of their families, people who have friends in New York that they can't find." She quickly and quietly relayed the story of the Bakers, her eyes filling in sympathy as she did so.

"Oh, those poor people," her mother said, and Abby could envision her shaking her head, her fingertips against her chin in her usual pose of concern. "I'm afraid New York is going to

92

lose a lot of her people. Even her emergency crews. Cops, fire-fighters, EMTs. It's so hard to fathom, Abby. We were all trying to wrap our brains around it last night as we watched the news. Thousands of people. *Thousands*. It's almost beyond comprehension."

They talked for a few more minutes, mostly about the confusion and inability to understand why somebody would do such a thing. Michelle told her New York was still a mess, people running around like chickens with their heads cut off (one of her favorite expressions) and that it would be weeks, maybe months, maybe longer before anything was even close to resembling "the way it was" before the eleventh. The sorrow in her voice was heartbreaking. For somebody who had grown up in New York, who considered the city to be in her blood, the recent events were akin to a death—or more accurately, a murder. Michelle and so many others like her had been plunged into a state of horrified, disbelieving grief.

Aware of the people waiting for the phones, Abby bid her mother goodbye, promising to call again soon. "I love you, Mom."

"Love you, too, baby. Stay safe."

Across the front lobby, Abby could see Corinne scurrying about like a small animal, handing out supplies, hugging a small boy, smiling reassuringly at a haggard-looking older woman. Shaking her head in awe, Abby wondered how the Gander native did it, how she kept smiling, kept helping, kept calm amidst the chaos that had become her quiet little town. If ever there was a walking, talking inspiration, Corinne MacDougal was it.

"Can I help?" Abby asked as she approached and took a large box of fruit out of Corinne's hands.

"Oh, Abby, thank you, dear. How are you today?"

"Hanging in there. What about you? Did you get any sleep last night? I barely saw you this morning before you were off again."

"I know. I'd napped a bit here yesterday, so I was fine. I wanted to get an early start because I knew Bill was bringing by more eggs and Bill Rigby is the earliest riser I've ever known." She said this in an affectionate tone and Abby absently wondered if any-body ever rubbed Corinne the wrong way.

"I hope you know how much we all," she made a gesture encompassing the whole area, "appreciate what you've done for us. I don't know what we'd all have done without your help."

Corinne scoffed and waved a dismissive hand, just as Abby expected she would.

"Listen, we're going to cook you dinner tonight."

"What? Oh, no."

"No arguing," Abby said. "You've been so great to us, it's the least we can do."

She fished around a bit about likes and dislikes, got directions to the nearest grocery store, then collected Brian and Michael and filled them in on her plan to make the MacDougals dinner. They both agreed heartily, not only because it was a nice thank you gesture but because it also gave them something to focus on for the rest of the day. Boredom was beginning to set in for all of them.

"Let's stop back at the house first and see if Erica wants to go with," Abby said from the backseat.

Brian snorted from his spot behind the wheel. "Really? She didn't seem to want anything to do with us earlier. Why do you think she'd change her mind now?"

Abby shrugged, looked out the window. "I don't know. I just think we should ask."

"I think she'd just as soon wish us all away. She's cold, that one."

"I don't know," Abby said again, leaving the rest of her thoughts unvoiced.

Michael spoke up from the passenger seat. "You know, Erica is very much like my younger sister, Claire." He was soft-spoken, causing Abby to sit forward in her seat to hear him, his accent almost musical. "She gets that from a lot of people who make snap judgments about her just from being around her for a day." He glanced at Brian. "No offense."

"None taken."

"Claire just isn't good around a lot of people. It drains her. She likes to be alone. She craves silence. It doesn't mean she's cold or a bitch or any of the other myriad things people label her. It's just who she is and those who know her and love her understand that. I think Erica is the same way. We just don't know her well enough to realize it."

Brian shrugged, making it clear what he thought of the analysis. Abby pursed her lips and absorbed Michael's words, nodding slightly.

"I'll just run in," Abby said as they pulled into the MacDougals' driveway. "Be right back."

She didn't know why she half-expected to find Erica on the couch in the living room watching TV. Maybe because that's where Abby herself would be? But the first floor was quiet. It wasn't until she entered the kitchen that she heard the strange hum and the rhythmic pounding sound—a steady thump-thump-thump filtering up from the basement. Her shoes made no sound as she descended the stairs and peeked around to her left. The sight stopped her in her tracks, sent her heart racing, and stole all moisture from her mouth.

The pounding was caused by Erica's sneakered feet hitting the base of Kate MacDougal's underused treadmill as she ran. Running wasn't something Abby had enjoyed in her life. Ever. She felt that it took all the fun out of an activity. She avoided sports like basketball and field hockey because they required too much running. She preferred volleyball. Maybe a little badminton. Golf was a good one. No running required. She never understood the "runner's high" her jogging friends spoke of, but looking at Erica now, she thought she almost got it. Her face was relaxed. Her body was working hard, but damn if she wasn't almost smiling. Navy blue shorts from Walmart hugged that muscular behind of hers and her simple white T-shirt was nearly soaked through. All the rich copper hair was pulled back into a ponytail and it flounced from side to side with each stride. Erica's pale skin glistened with perspiration, her arms pumped in an easy rhythm, and Abby realized that Erica ran often. She looked so at ease, so relaxed that Abby hated to interrupt her. Instead, she stood quietly and watched for several moments, wondering if, in Erica's mind, she was running *from* something or *to* something.

95

Then she tried to remember the last time she'd seen anything quite so sexy.

Back in the car, she told the guys, "Nope. She's busy. Let's go."

Brian wanted to ask why her cheeks were all flushed, but thought better of it.

Chapter 10

Erica felt reborn. De-stressed, centered. She often forgot how much a good run could reboot her system. Something about the adrenaline, the pumping blood, the sweat made her feel alive again. And with the feel of life came the perception of control, whether real or imagined. Running always left her feeling grounded and in charge. She came up the basement steps, ready to face people again, just as Brian, Michael, and Abby were hauling grocery bags in from the car. Abby took in the black workout pants and the baby blue shirt and blurted, "How many outfits did you buy the other day? Wasn't I with you the whole time?"

"This is my last one," Erica said. "Remind me to ask Corinne if she'd mind if we did some laundry tonight. I can throw all of our stuff in together and I'm sure we'd have a good-sized load." She noticed the bags and asked, "What's going on?"

"I thought we could make dinner for Corinne and Tim," Abby said, trying hard not to stare. Erica had obviously showered, her ponytail still damp, and she smelled like baby powder. "As sort of a thank you, small as it is, for all they've done for us."

"That's a great idea. What are we having?" She peered into the bags as the guys deposited them onto the kitchen counter and went to grab the last of the bunch.

"Chicken, potatoes, corn," Abby rattled off.

"Cool. How are we cooking the chicken?"

"No idea."

"What?"

"I have no idea, but I think Michael does."

"You decided to cook for somebody, but . . ."

Abby nodded sheepishly. "I don't cook."

Erica burst into laughter. "Why am I not surprised?" She shook her head, then began taking things out of the bags and setting them on the counter, checking her resources and seeing what she had to work with. She opened a few of Corinne's cupboards, the fridge, checking for spices and seasonings, then gave one nod of approval as the guys set down the last two bags. "What time will the MacDougals be home?"

"I said we'd be ready to eat by six?" Abby phrased it as a question, her expression hopeful.

"Okay. We can work with this, no problem."

"Wait, you can cook?" Abby asked.

"I can."

"Why am I surprised?"

Erica shot her a mysteriously sexy grin, shrugged, and began gathering her ingredients. Michael offered his assistance, promising he knew his way around a kitchen, so Erica took him up on it. Abby and Brian would be sous chefs. It was after four, so Erica decided there was plenty of time to bake the chicken. Mashed potatoes and seasoned corn rounded out the menu. There were also ingredients for a salad.

"All right. Abby, you are the Salad Queen. You can make one big one or six individuals. Up to you. Brian, you get to be Mr. Potato Head. Can you peel and dice those potatoes? They need to go into a big pot of water, which you'll have to find first."

"I'm all over it." He began searching cupboards and pantries.

"Michael, I'm pretty sure there was some fresh rosemary wrapped up in the fridge and I need the butter in the door."

"Right-o."

"And correct me if I'm wrong, but did I see a bag that had wine in it?" She raised her eyebrows in hopeful question.

"You did," Brian responded, finding said bag.

"All chefs need to have a glass while they work," she instructed.

"My mom always has a glass while she's cooking," Abby confirmed with a nod.

Brian pulled out four bottles, two red and two white. "And if it sucks, blame the British guy. Abby and I were at a loss."

Michael grinned at Erica. "I assure you, it will not suck. Trust me."

"How do I not trust a guy who sounds like James Bond?" Erica asked, feigning bewilderment.

The four of them worked like a well-oiled machine, Brian peeling and chopping, Abby slicing and tossing, Michael following Erica's instructions regarding the corn, and Erica treating the chicken to a savory-smelling rosemary and olive oil rub. They talked about their afternoons, teased one another playfully, and essentially felt like one big family, akin to siblings home for the holidays. By the time Corinne walked in at five-thirty, the kitchen was filled with delicious aromas, laughter, and lively conversation.

"Oh, my, it smells divine in here," she exclaimed, setting her purse on the bench by the side door.

"Where's Tim?" Michael asked her.

"Oh, I decided I could use some fresh air after being inside so long, so I walked."

"You walked? We could have come to get you."

Corinne waved a dismissive hand. "Not at all. It did me good."

Brian held up two wine bottles for her to see. "Red or white?"

Erica laughed and shook her head. "He means Merlot or Pinot Grigio."

"White," Corinne replied.

"I'm surrounded by Neanderthals!"

Corinne laughed and took the glass Brian poured for her. "How are things at the Club?" he asked.

A sip of the wine seemed to visibly relax her and she exhaled heavily. "People are restless. Of course. They want to go home. And those poor Bakers." She tsk'd, her expression sympathetic.

"Still nothing about their son?" Abby asked.

"Not a word. Nobody's been able to get in touch with him, though their daughter did find out that some of his colleagues are safe."

"That's good," Brian said.

"I think so, too." They absorbed that quietly for a moment

before Corinne changed the subject. "It's so wonderful of you to cook for us."

"Please," Abby said. "It's the least we can do. You've been so amazing to us."

"This whole town has," Michael added. "Did you know we had to force the gentleman at the grocer to take our money?"

"You did?" Erica asked, surprised.

"He wanted to just give it to us."

"My god," she said, utterly awed by the generosity. "The phone company, the pharmacy, now the grocery store." She turned to Corinne, hoping she could see the gratitude she felt. "The people of Gander are something else. Truly. I'm stunned by the kindness and generosity we've run into here." With a half-grin, she added, "And I'm not easily stunned. By anybody."

Corinne shrugged, her expression telling them it was no big deal, like this was how her fellow townsfolk were all the time, like it would never occur to them to handle the situation any differently.

Tim arrived about ten minutes later, forgoing a glass of wine for a beer and by 6:15, the six of them were seated around the dining-room table, a veritable feast laid out in front of them.

"I'd like to propose a toast," Michael announced, raising his glass. "To the MacDougals, for taking in four complete strangers at a time of crisis and providing them with beds, showers, food and drink, and the comforts of home while they're all so far away from their own. Your hospitality is so much more than 'appreciated.' Thank you."

"Hear, hear," Abby added.

They clinked glasses as Corinne and Tim blushed at the praise, and then dug into the food—which was delicious if the moans of pleasure were any indication.

"Oh, my god, Erica," Brian said around a mouthful of chicken. "This is incredible."

"You weren't kidding when you said you could cook," Abby said with a wink. "Wow."

A little self-conscious, Erica smiled at the compliment. She'd forgotten how satisfying it could be to cook for others. Maddie had loved to throw dinner parties and Erica found cooking to be a good way to not have to socialize with the six or seven people in her living room; it was a built-in excuse to stay in the kitchen, and she used it whenever she could. The fact that she got good at cooking—and also began to enjoy doing it—was simply a bonus.

They ate and talked and laughed. They shared wine and stories of their lives and Erica was shocked at how much they felt like a family. How could that happen in three days? How could she feel so close to these people—people she essentially knew nothing about? She was not a person who settled in easily. She was uncomfortable more often than not and when they'd first arrived at the MacDougal house, she'd been sure she'd be certifiably insane within twenty-four hours. Yet here she sat, breaking bread at the dinner table of a couple she barely knew and feeling more comfortable than she had in weeks. Months even. It was as close as she'd felt to being at home with her family in longer than she cared to think about. The realization brought an unexpected surge of emotion and her eyes misted even as a gentle smile crossed her lips.

Abby had not allowed them to leave the grocery store without dessert: ice cream. Four kinds, as she didn't know who liked what. Chocolate, vanilla, mint chocolate chip, and black cherry. They all protested that they had no room left after such an incredible dinner, but they all ate a bowl. By seven, the six of them were slouched in their chairs.

"I can't move," Brian said, holding his belly like a pregnant woman.

"Me, neither," Abby agreed. "I'm thinking the second bowl of ice cream? Not a great idea."

"I might have to sleep in this chair," Tim said with a chuckle.

They continued to chat, reluctant to have the meal come to an end. But Corinne wanted to get back to the Lions Club, where she thought she might spend the night so the Bakers had constant company. Tim had rounds to make, checking on supplies for other emergency housing locations. Erica offered to do a load of laundry and the other three volunteered for clean-up duty.

Another half-hour went by before anybody got up from the table.

ভ ভ ভ

Folding clothes had always relaxed Erica. She supposed it wasn't all that unusual; lots of people used some sort of chore as a stress reliever. Her mom liked to reorganize her spice cupboard, and her dad always told her that doing inventory at the feed store calmed him. Erica felt that way about laundry. Something about the tidiness of folding a shirt, of stacking panties or pairing up socks, always made her feel better, like she had the situation under control.

She piled all the guys' clothes together on the stripped bed—and there weren't many—to let them sort through and divide. She absently wondered who wore the tightie-whities and who had the silk boxers, but she wasn't about to ask. In the other pile were Abby's clothes and her clothes; again, neither of them had much. She did know that the cotton boy shorts were not hers and her brain kept trying to help her picture Abby in them, despite her resistance. Not an unpleasant image, that was for sure.

As if on cue, Abby came bounding down the basement stairs, grinning like always.

"Hey," she said, flopping onto the bare mattress.

"Hey," Erica replied, folding the last T-shirt in the pile.

"I'm exhausted."

"Me, too. It's past my bedtime."

Abby gestured toward the laundry with her eyes. "Need some help?"

With a poignant glance and an arched brow, Erica surveyed the neatly folded clothing. "Your timing is impeccable."

"You're not the first person to say so."

"Shocking. How was the poker game?" Erica hated playing cards, and she had no idea how to play poker, but the other three were big fans of it. Tim and Corinne had some plastic chips lying around and the trio had used them for betting money.

"I was up fifty bucks!"

"And then?"

"Michael took me to the cleaners. I'm broke. And he gets my firstborn."

"The bastard."

"Right? You've got to watch out for those quiet ones with the charming accents. They're trouble."

"Well, Trouble's laundry is done. Could you run it up there? And when you come back, you can help me make the bed. The sheets should be dry by now."

By the time Erica had moved their clean clothes to the loveseat and retrieved the sheets from the dryer, Abby had returned. She took her place on the opposite side of the bed and caught her end of the fitted sheet when Erica flipped it to her. She inhaled deeply.

"Ahhhhh. Boy, there's nothing like the smell of clean sheets."

"And they're still warm." They worked together and got the fitted sheet in place. Erica unfurled the flat sheet. She wet her lips and kept her eyes focused on the task at hand. "Um, I've been thinking. There's no reason either of us should have to sleep on the loveseat. It's too short and I'm sure it's not terribly comfortable, and this bed is plenty big. Do you mind sharing?"

The surprise zipped across Abby's face before she could catch it, and she was pretty sure Erica saw it. But she covered it with a smile. "I don't mind at all."

"Good." Erica tossed a pillow and a pillow case to Abby and they both put one inside the other. "I think dinner went over well."

"Yeah? Well, you're a hell of a cook."

Erica waved her off. "It was a good idea. And a very nice one."

Abby felt her cheeks heat up a bit. "I just, I believe in giving what you get. I wanted to repay them somehow, you know?"

"I know. It was a good thing."

"This is all so crazy," Abby said as they finished and sat on the end of the bed. "I'm having a hard time wrapping my brain around it."

Erica blew out a breath. "Me, too."

Abby turned to look at her. "You know, Brian was totally right.

This is going to be like JFK's assassination. Everybody who was alive that day can remember exactly where they were when they heard the news. Now we have that, too."

Erica nodded slowly, realizing the truth of Abby's words. "Where were you when the towers came down?" she asked softly.

"Exactly."

"It's weird."

"It totally is. And it breaks my heart."

They got ready for bed in silence, working around each other as if they'd been living together for years—handing over a toothbrush, reaching in front of the other for a towel, a gentle hand on a hip as one moved behind the other. Light was extinguished and they climbed into bed, each on her own side, both lying on their backs, looking up at the drop ceiling, lost in thought.

Abby was just starting to drift off when Erica spoke, her voice just above a whisper. "You know what I have the hardest time with?"

"What?"

"This thing that happened—no, wait. It didn't happen. It was done. Somebody did it. It's not something that happened, it's something that was done. This thing that was done is the perfect example of evil, right? Wouldn't you agree? People who are pure evil did this."

"Okay."

"In the midst of this terrible thing that was done, smack dab in the middle of all the horror and chaos, we meet some of the most wonderfully kind and giving people on the planet." She paused and Abby could hear her swallow. "If not for the most evil, despicable people in the world, I would never have met some of the most generous and loving people in the world. I—I don't— what am I supposed to do with that?"

Beneath the covers, Abby grabbed Erica's hand and entwined their fingers, hoping the contact would help alleviate the crack in Erica's voice. "I don't know," she whispered.

"I'm not even sure I've ever experienced pure goodness before."

"Never?"

"No. Not pure, unexpectant goodness. Real, honest-to-god grace. With no strings attached. I feel like Tim and Corinne are the poster children to represent that. So many people here in Gander represent that. And yet, it took pure, unadulterated evil to show me that goodness." She spat a humorless laugh. "Is it some kind of cosmic joke?"

Abby smiled in the dark. "I have no idea, but it reminds me of my great-grandma, who always used to say 'God never closes a door without opening a window.' Now, I'm not at all a religious person and I don't imagine you are either, given that you work in the field of science, but I do believe in the Universe and I do believe that things happen for a reason, even horrible things." Erica could feel her shrug. "Maybe we were meant to be here. Maybe I was supposed to run into Corinne and Tim and the Bakers and Brian and Michael." She squeezed. "And you. Maybe in all of this mess, we were supposed to meet."

Erica wanted to scoff at the suggestion of destiny, wanted to scream, I don't understand! But Abby sounded so real. So convinced. She didn't have the heart to burst her bubble. So she squeezed back and said simply, "Maybe."

ભ ભ ભ

At 12:37, Erica was still wide awake. Not because she wanted to be, but because her head wouldn't allow her to ignore the fact that there was a warm, soft, femininely attractive body sleeping soundly next to her. Not just any body. Abby's body. She'd been so bound and determined to dislike her that she barely noticed how much Abby had been growing on her until it was too late. Now, she lay in Kate MacDougal's bed, her own body on red alert, her skin aware of every cell and fiber that even came close to making contact with Abby.

Erica's eyes had grown accustomed to the dark long ago. While she was silently counting ceiling tiles and listening to the guys close up shop on the first floor and head up to bed them-selves, Abby had fallen immediately asleep, her deep and even breathing giving Erica the high sign that the coast was clear. She turned her head and studied the woman next to her. Pollyanna, she thought with a grin that felt almost tender.

In the darkness, Abby lay on her back, one hand resting on her abdomen on top of the blankets, the other curled in a loose fist against her temple. Erica could make out the planes of her face, even the smoothness of her skin. The dark brows seemed expertly placed for maximum emphasis of those incredible eyes— eyes it was probably a good thing Erica couldn't see right now, or she might do something, unwise. Abby's nose was very straight with little curve to its bridge. Her hand was small, her fingers long and tapered, the nails trimmed and filed smooth. Strong hands. Feminine hands. Hands that would—Erica swallowed hard, pulling her thoughts away from the subject, though she knew herself well enough to know she'd revisit it again before the night was over. It had been too long and she was finding Abby far too attractive not to at least think about it.

Sex with Maddie had been good. It had been satisfying and fun and Erica hoped that Maddie'd felt the same way. That being said, there was still something that Erica felt she was missing. She'd never been able to put her finger on it, to give it a word, to describe it accurately. Something akin to rawness, to aching need. She'd never needed sex with Maddie. She'd simply wanted it. And that had been enough. For a while.

Once the sex stopped, the entire relationship had fallen apart. To this day, Erica wasn't exactly sure why that had happened. Her job had picked up. Could it have really been that simple? Her hours got longer and so her relationship ended? She had to believe it was already doomed by then. Their time together became less and less, and when they did see each other, Erica had been so exhausted that she fell right to sleep. By the time she understood there was a real problem, Maddie had accused her of being cold and unavailable, and that was the end of that.

I'm not cold. Am I? It was a discussion she'd had with herself more times than she could count. She'd wonder if she was un-approachable, if she came off as aloof to others. But she was a good conversationalist. She knew that. She could hold up her end of a discussion with no problem. She was fun to talk to. *Wasn't she?* The old demons from high school would rear their ugly heads just long enough to allow insecurity to creep in. It wasn't as if she didn't have any friends. She did. Only a handful of them were important to her. It wasn't as if she hadn't had her share of women—or men, for that matter—interested in her. There had been plenty. She was just choosy.

Inches from getting swallowed up by the vicious circle of her thoughts, she felt Abby shift in her sleep. She turned from her back onto her stomach and slipped her bare leg over Erica's, the warm skin acting more like ice, shocking Erica even more awake than she had been. Erica caught her bottom lip between her teeth and sucked in a breath, stunned by the smoothness of the skin, realizing Abby, too, had found fit to use the plastic razor in the shower.

"Jesus," she said aloud, wondering at the sudden dampness of her panties. When had she become such a guy? When had she become so easily turned on? And then—as if it had a mind of its own—her hand reached down and laid itself across the side of Abby's knee. Gently, softly, her palm rested against warm, silky skin. Just rested there. No rubbing. No squeezing. Just contact. Comforting, delicious contact.

Abby didn't move, didn't shift, slept on.

Erica sighed with a contentment she hadn't felt in months, possibly longer.

And finally, she slept.

107

September 14, 2001
Friday

Chapter 11

Mixed emotions were not something Abby Hayes handled well. She didn't like the confusion, the uncertainty. She liked to be steady and sure, to understand what she was thinking and feeling and why.

This was not going to be a morning for such certainty. She knew that as soon as she'd opened her eyes to find herself completely wrapped around Erica's sleeping body, spooning with her like they'd been sharing a bed for years.

Abby sipped her coffee and tried to expunge the image, the memory, from her mind. It was very early and she was alone on the MacDougals' back patio curled up in a lounge chair she'd wiped free of dew. Waiting for the sunrise was something she loved doing, had always done no matter where she was. It made her feel alive and ready to face a new day. This morning wasn't about that, though. It was simply about getting away from the bed, getting away from the body that taunted her because she knew if she stayed, she'd test her theory about how easy it might be to push Erica's T-shirt up and reveal those beautiful breasts; how little effort it would take to slip her hand down the front of Erica's panties; how quickly she could wake up her bunkmate and have her breathing raggedly, clinging to Abby's shoulders and begging for release.

Hot coffee slopped over the rim of her mug and splashed onto her hand as Abby shook her head vigorously in the hopes of dislodging such scenes and letting them fall away. She winced, welcoming the pain, welcoming anything that would take her mind off how well she'd slept curled around Erica, off what she wanted to do to her under the covers.

Those feelings were only part of the mixed emotions.

The rest came from the dreams she'd had, dreams that most likely stemmed from all her interaction with the Bakers as well as other Plane People, along with the news reports she'd seen and heard. In her dreams, it was her mother she worried about. All night long, Abby dreamed that horrible things had befallen her. Once, she was missing. Another time, she was jumping out the window of a thirty-third story window and plunging to her death as Abby watched helplessly, screaming. Yet another dream showed Michelle Hayes falling to the ground as mounds of cement blocks and dusty rubble buried her alive, only her hand sticking out, reaching in vain for help.

If Abby had been in bed alone, she'd have gotten up hours earlier, paced the house, watched TV. But each time she jerked awake, the warmth of Erica's body soothed her, made her feel safe. One time, she woke up to find herself curled against Erica's back, her arm draped over Erica's stomach. As she tried to extricate herself, Erica grabbed on in her sleep and snuggled her butt back against Abby's middle, virtually gluing them together. Abby had relaxed immediately and drifted back into oblivion until 5:15, when she decided she couldn't stand the images any longer and slipped quietly—and somewhat regretfully—from the warm cocoon of the bed.

Worry. Fear, anger, anguish. All these emotions warred within her and it wasn't a feeling Abby liked. She was a cheerful person, a person who saw the bright side of things, a person whose cup was always half full—the eternal optimist. She was the person that picked up spiders and put them outside instead of killing them. She helped worms struggling across hot sidewalks make it to the grass so they wouldn't fry. It drove some of her friends crazy, but made most of them happy to be around her. But this—this—event. This horror. This surrealistic thing that had taken her home, her city, her country by surprise had knocked her for a loop. She felt off-balance, like life had tipped sideways and was sliding out of place and there was no way she could catch everything and keep it from becoming hopelessly discombobulated, forever scrambled, and never, ever the same again. She'd spent the past couple of days clinging desperately to her optimism, trying hard to keep everybody else up and smiling and positive, but the truth was, she was running out of steam. She was exhausted and she was scared. She was worried about her mother. She was worried about her father—on a business trip and stranded in Phoenix, her mother told her. She was worried about her mother's friends. She was worried about Tyson Baker. She was worried about Tyson's parents and how they would handle losing him—because that was the reality and both she and the Bakers knew it deep down, beneath their hope and their prayers. At this point, the chances of Tyson still being alive were slim. Very slim.

Tears pooled in her eyes and she wiped at them in frustration.

How could this happen?

How could this happen?

It was the thought on everybody's mind, she was sure of it. How could this possibly happen? And why? What had we done to deserve this? There wasn't an official body count yet, but the twin towers had one hundred ten stories each. It was going to be thousands. Just like that. In one fell swoop. Did we deserve such agony? Such heartache? Did anybody?

Abby's brain cramped with the inability to take in something so incomprehensible.

She pulled her knees up to her chin, wrapped her arms around them in an effort to ward off the chill suddenly enveloping her.

She missed her mother.

ରେ ଓଃ ରେ

Erica was a sound sleeper, always had been. She rarely had trouble sleeping away from her own bed and the MacDougals' house was no exception; she slept like a baby in the big bed in the basement. Soft laughter bubbled up as she spoke the thought aloud.

"Big bed in the basement."

113

What was that grouping of words called? She wracked her brain until she came up with the right title: alliteration. She'd always done well in English class.

She stretched her arms over her head and yawned widely, feeling completely rested. The emptiness of the space next to her brought foggy memories to her brain—warmth, comfort, an arm wrapped protectively around her middle. Unable to grasp anything more solid than that, she thought, *And there's the drawback to being such a sound sleeper.* She couldn't recall more than a few fleeting images, but those she did remember gave her a weird tingle. The bed next to her was cool and she wondered how long ago Abby had left it. Surprised, she realized she missed Abby's face. The absence of that perpetually cheerful smile, which Erica had wanted to slap off more than once over the past couple of days, left an empty space that felt . . . wrong, somehow.

The subtle smell of coffee drifted temptingly down the stairs, giving her an idea where her roommate had gone and creating enough incentive to get her out of bed. She threw on the same clothes she'd worn two days ago—since they were now clean and smelled good—pulled her hair back into a ponytail, and headed up to the kitchen with an idea.

A quick peek out the kitchen window told her Tim had either come home late and left early or hadn't come home at all, as his car was not in the driveway. Corinne was planning on staying overnight at the Lions Club, so she assumed the four Plane People were once again alone in the MacDougals' house. The car keys to the second car sat on the counter where Corinne had left them last night after dinner, giving them explicit instructions not to hesitate to use them. Again, Erica shook her head with amused disbelief at the trust the couple had in them. There was no way in a million years she'd ever let four complete strangers camp out in her apartment, eat all her food, have unlimited access to her car, *especially* if she wasn't even there. But Tim and Corinne seemed honestly happy to have them and Erica felt this weird, sudden urge to be extra respectful, like a twelve-year-old wanting to be on her best behavior.

Erica pulled what she needed from the refrigerator, found the right pans, and got to work. It wasn't long before the smell of bacon had Brian stumbling sleepily down the stairs. Michael followed close behind him.

"Oh, man, is there a better smell in the world?" he asked, filling two mugs with coffee and handing one over to Michael. "I think even a vegetarian must be able to appreciate the smell of bacon."

"I am very fond of breakfast," Michael said matter-of-factly.

"Me, too," Erica agreed. "My favorite dinners with my parents were always when we had breakfast, usually on Friday nights. My mom would make French toast or omelets or pancakes."

"I like that idea," Brian said.

"You've never done that?"

"I don't think so. But I'm going to institute it when I get back home."

Erica grinned at him. "Yeah?"

"Breakfast for Dinner Fridays. A new tradition in the Caldwell household."

"Traditions are good."

"You're invited over any time."

"To Wisconsin?"

"Any time."

Erica flipped the bacon, glanced at him. "It's a haul from North Carolina, but you never know, I may take you up on that."

"It's a standing invitation." He turned to Michael, who'd taken a seat at the small kitchen table. "For you, too, man."

Michael smiled warmly. "Thank you."

"Hey, where's Abby?" He looked around as if she might be standing in the corner and he'd just missed her.

"I was wondering the same thing," Erica said as she used tongs to remove the bacon from the pan and set it on paper towels to drain. "She must have gotten out of the bed pretty early, but I was sleeping hard and didn't feel her leave."

Brian shot a look to Michael, who pressed his lips together and looked away.

"But the coffee is still fairly fresh, so she couldn't have left that long ago," Erica continued, oblivious to the silent conversation going on between the two men behind her. She hadn't actively searched for Abby because as she cooked, those fleeting images from earlier had begun to solidify in her head until she was reasonably sure they'd spent much of the night curled up into each other. She wasn't sure what to do with that. Nor was she sure how to deal with the tiny ember of arousal that burned in the pit of her stomach when she thought about it.

Talking to Abby about it was probably the thing to do. It was also the thing that terrified her most at the moment. So she focused on breakfast.

"How do you guys like your eggs?"

About a half-hour later, the three of them were finishing up their breakfasts in the dining room when Abby came in through the back door. Erica looked up, surprised to see her, then immediately concerned about the pink around her eyes, the worry etched across her face.

"Hey, there you are," Erica said, forcing a pleasant tone into her voice. "Are you okay?"

Abby visibly pulled herself together and held up her mug. "I'm on empty. And I couldn't avoid the bacon any longer."

"I saved you a couple of pieces." Erica got up and took the mug. As she filled it, she asked softly, "How do you like your eggs?"

Abby had intended to sneak downstairs and not bother the other three, but something in Erica's blue eyes—something warm and surprisingly tender—kept her riveted to the kitchen floor, wouldn't let her leave. A quick flash of being pressed against Erica's back sent her body temperature through the roof.

"And don't tell me you're not hungry," Erica gently scolded before Abby could protest breakfast.

"Over easy?" Abby said, not bothering to fight.

"You got it." She handed the coffee to Abby and studied her for a moment. The usual cheerfulness, the perpetual exuberance was strangely subdued, making Erica squint in subtle confusion.

Abby somehow managed not to jump in surprise when Erica reached out and stroked her cheek with a thumb. "Are you sure you're okay?"

Abby swallowed hard, willing her eyes not to drift shut at the touch. "Yeah. I'm fine. Just—" She tapped her temple with a finger. "Too much going on."

Erica nodded and went to work on the eggs.

Abby wasn't the only one somewhat subdued, Erica noticed as they sat down. Brian and Michael remained seated, so Abby didn't have to eat alone, but nobody had much to say. The inconvenience of being stranded combined with the horror of what had happened in New York was starting to weigh on everybody. Erica found herself in the unfamiliar position of keeping the conversation going in a group. If her friends hadn't looked so glum, she might have found amusement over the prospect.

Her *friends*—that's how she thought of them. It was a foreign feeling to her. Not that she'd made friends, but that she'd made them in so short a time—less than three days, really. She felt an inexplicable, unbreakable bond with these three people—and the MacDougals as well—who had been strangers to her on Tuesday. Now here she was, on Friday of the same week, and she knew in her heart she'd do anything any one of them asked of her, no question.

The realization both warmed her insides and threw her off-balance.

"I was thinking of heading over to the Lions Club this morning, see if Corinne could use some help." Erica looked around the table. "Anybody want to tag along?"

"I'm going to go for a run," Michael said as he stood and took his dishes into the kitchen. "Thank you, though."

"It's time I sat down and watched the news," Brian said soberly. "I've been trying to avoid it, but now I feel like, I feel like I need to see it. I need to see it all." He didn't look like it was something he *wanted* to do, but Erica didn't try to talk him out of it. Maybe he was right. Maybe he needed to see it, though why, she had no idea.

117

Abby barely looked up from her plate on which she'd been mostly pushing her eggs around. "I'm—no. Thanks, but no. I'll stay here."

Chapter 12

The Plane People had been understandably restless since shortly after their flights were diverted on Tuesday, but by Friday they were starting to go stir-crazy. Tempers were short. Close quarters had become unbearably close. The news reports had more and more detail to share, which made emotions run high. Despite the best efforts and endless generosity of the residents of Gander, most people wanted nothing more than to go home.

Erica could feel the change in the atmosphere the second she stepped into the Lions Club. The air felt thick with stress, like she could reach out and touch it, examine it from various angles. A small boy—not more than four years old—ran past her as fast as his legs would carry him. His mother trailed after him, not even close to catching him, looking exhausted. Erica wondered how many times they'd played this game and exactly how long ago Mom had had enough.

Corinne spotted her first, gave a genuine smile, and waved her over. She had to be just as wiped out—if not more so—as everybody there, but she looked unflappable, fresh and cheerful, as if there was no place in the world she'd rather be. She rubbed Erica's arm affectionately.

"Hello there, stranger. How are you today?" Her voice was slightly hoarse.

"I'm good," Erica replied. "How are you? You sound like you're coming down with something."

Corinne waved her off. "Oh, no. I'm fine. How are your cohorts?"

Erica thought back to her fellow houseguests, the tired, unanimated expressions on their faces when she left. "Good.

Everybody's pooped, I think." She shrugged and held her hands out to her sides in presentation. "You've got me. What can I do?"

For the next several hours, Erica stopped thinking and did whatever Corinne needed. She gathered dirty towels from the bathroom and set them aside to be picked up and laundered. She wandered the room full of Plane People with a wicker basket of snack-sized bags—potato chips, pretzels, Doritos, cookies—to see if anybody was hungry. She ran a dust mop over the floor of the lobby area. She counted various toiletry items for Corinne's inventory sheet, so they knew what more to order.

It felt good. And Erica was surprised by that. She felt like she was contributing, like she was helping the situation run more smoothly. Volunteering was new to her; she'd never done it before and she liked it. She was almost embarrassed to realize she was proud of herself.

A middle-aged woman with small, birdlike features approached the food table and perused her choices. Catching Corinne's eye, she asked, "Is it true? About the Lufthansa flight? Did they get to go home?"

Erica's ears perked up. Home? Somebody was going home? Was it finally happening?

"That flight went back to Germany, I believe," Corinne said, furrowing her brow.

"So, they're clearing flights?"

"I don't know, dear. I honestly don't. But Carl Sullivan will be here shortly and he might have information. I'll be sure to ask him."

The woman nodded, then hovered, wanting to be sure that was all the detail she'd get. Once she left, Erica caught Corinne's eye.

"That flight went back to Germany," Corinne said in a low voice. "But they were telling people they were going to Dallas. I think they just wanted to get everybody back on the plane. From what I understand, there were seven Americans who refused to get on the plane after being lied to about the destination."

"I don't blame them," Erica said.

"Neither do I. But now they have to find their own way home."

"Well, that sucks."

Corinne barked a laugh at Erica's matter-of-fact tone. "It does, doesn't it? As if they weren't dealing with enough stress already. Now they have to try to rent a car or something? There aren't any." She shook her head and tsk'd.

Erica remembered hearing that people from the first couple of flights that deplaned on Tuesday, mostly business folk who were well-schooled in such things, had made a run on Gander's rental car places and every last vehicle had been taken, leaving the rest of the passengers at the mercy of the airlines.

"Do you think they'll start clearing flights soon?" she asked Corinne.

"I don't know. From what I've heard, American airspace is still closed. The flights that have been cleared are heading back to Europe."

Erica nodded and managed to stifle a sigh. She envied the people headed back to Europe, if for no other reason than they were moving, they were no longer stranded, stuck in limbo.

As if reading her thoughts, Corinne touched her shoulder warmly. "Don't worry. It won't be long." Her kind eyes were soft and Erica immediately felt guilty.

"Not that Gander hasn't been wonderful," she said, trying to clarify.

"There's no place like home. I understand that, believe me."

"That's the truth." Although when Erica's mind thought of home, it went to Illinois, to her parents' house, to the feed store, not to her apartment in North Carolina, not to her office. *Weird.*

Tucking her hands against her hips, Erica looked around, wondering what she could do next. Noticing her scanning the area, Corinne gave her a gentle push. "Sweetie, go outside and get some air. It's a beautiful day out and you've been a huge help to me. Go enjoy a little sunshine. Might not be here long, you know."

Erica was no stranger to the fickleness of autumn in the north.

Growing up in Illinois, she'd seen her share of strange weather, of freak storms, of what seemed like weeks of no sun. She took Corinne up on her offer and headed outside.

The air was cooler than it had been, but it felt good on Erica's skin. Even a refrigerator would end up feeling stuffy and hot if there were 200-plus people wandering around in it for four days. She inhaled deeply, tasting the ocean's salt on the gentle breeze.

People were milling around, wandering like souls with no direction. Three people sat on a curb while their children chased each other in some toddler version of tag. To Erica's left, two women were chatting while one took a cigarette break.

"Cutest damn thing," the blond nonsmoker said. "Cocker spaniel puppy. Can't be more than five or six months old. All ears. Ralph. Is that the cutest name you've ever heard for a puppy? My god, I just want to eat him up."

"What happened?" the smoker asked.

"I was looking in on him just after lunch yesterday and he just didn't seem right, you know? He was kind of listless. He wouldn't eat. His back end seemed a little tender. The poor thing. I got worried. I mean, how do you tell one of the Plane People, 'Gee, sorry you were stranded here for days on end, and by the way, your dog's dead?' I was really worried. So I called Doc Gallagher to come take a look."

"Oh, he's so nice. My Duke just loves going to vet appointments with him." Smoker took a long drag of her cigarette, released the smoke. Erica wrinkled her nose. "What'd he say?"

"Well, he came right out to the hangar and he looked Ralph all over. He said nothing seemed wrong, but he wanted to run some tests, just to be sure, because something didn't seem right."

"He ran tests right there?"

"Nope."

"But the animals aren't supposed to leave the hangar, are they?"

"Nope." At this, Blondie gave a conspiratorial smirk. "He snuck him out in a duffel bag!"

Erica knew all the animals from the planes were being housed in one of the hangars at the airport in a sort of quarantine. She couldn't imagine how hard it would be not to be able to have her dog with her during this time, but precautions had to be taken when it came to plants and animals entering from another country.

"He ran a bunch of tests," Blondie went on. "And couldn't find anything wrong with him. While he was gone, I asked around, asked all the other volunteers if they'd noticed anything strange about Ralph and you know what I found out?"

"Tell me!" Smoker was hanging on every word, as was Erica. *What's wrong with Ralph?!* her mind shrieked.

"Not only was the daytime crew of volunteers taking him out of his crate and playing with him, so was the *nighttime* crew! The poor little guy was *totally exhausted!*"

"Oh, my god. You're kidding."

"Swear," Blondie said, crossing her heart. "When Doc Gallagher snuck him back in, we both had a good laugh. And then I put poor Ralphie right into his crate with a clean, warm blanket and I made signs to hang around the area. *Please do not wake Ralph up to play with him. He's a growing boy who needs his sleep.*"

"Absolutely precious," Smoker said, stubbing out her cigarette in the nearby outdoor ashtray.

"You should come by and see him. But not if he's sleeping."

They both chuckled as they went back into the Lions Club. Erica found herself standing there with a big grin on her face as she pictured Ralph the cocker spaniel puppy curled up in a ball on a fluffy blanket. She loved animals, had always wanted a dog, in fact. But she worked long hours and never thought it would be fair to an animal to leave it alone for so long. How comforting it would be to have something waiting at home for her, though.

Ralph . . .

Still grinning, she went back inside to see what else Corinne might need.

But first she remembered to ask her what the damn cat's name was.

"Sammy," Corinne had said. "He doesn't like anybody. I'm

surprised you've seen him at all. He usually just hides behind the dryer."

Erica smiled.

ରେ   ରେ   ରେ

It was after six by the time Erica returned to the MacDougals' house. Corinne was planning to be at the Lions Club until later that night and Tim was just pulling out as Erica arrived. He rolled down his window as she approached, having parked Corinne's car on the street.

"Hey, there," he said with his ever-present grin.

"Hi, Tim."

"Corinne said she put you to work today, eh?"

"I was happy to help," Erica said and was somewhat surprised to realize that she meant it. "And it's the least I can do to repay you for all you've done for us."

"Bah." He dismissed her comment with a wave of his meaty hand.

"The others inside?"

At that, his face became a bit more serious. "Yeah. I'm afraid they've had a bit too much news reporting." He shook his head. "It's all so crazy, isn't it? Hard to fathom."

"That's for sure."

They parted ways, Tim off to see if they needed anything at the high school, Erica inside to check on her compadres, wondering if they'd had dinner.

Tim was right. They'd had too much news for one day. All three of them sat in the living room. Actually, *sat* was the wrong word; *sprawled* was more like it. Michael was on the couch with Brian, both of them slouched down on their spines like rag dolls. Abby was on the floor with Corinne's throw pillows bunched under her head. Each of them was pale and glassy-eyed, as if they hadn't seen sunshine in weeks. Erica was slightly taken aback by the changes in their demeanors in less than a day, and she had to stop and get her bearings before she spoke.

"Hey, guys," she said.

She was answered by a couple of grunts from the guys, nothing from Abby. She flopped down into a wingback chair with a relieved sigh. "Man, I worked my tail off today. I'm not sure how Corinne and the other volunteers are keeping up. There's so much to do and they're not getting much sleep."

Three sets of eyes stared at the television.

"Some of the flights that came from Europe are being cleared to head back there. We may be able to get out of here soon."

Nothing.

One last try, she thought, tamping down the irritation that was making itself known. "Did you guys eat? I'm starving. I can make us something."

Abby finally rolled over and faced her, but her expression was different. So not what Erica pictured when she thought of Abby. Not gentle. Not kind. Not cheerful. Instead, she was angry. Annoyed. Pissed off.

"What the hell's the matter with you?" she spat in Erica's direction.

Erica flinched as if she'd been slapped. "I'm sorry?"

"You heard me. What's wrong with you? Why are you suddenly so cheerful? Do you have any idea what's happening at home? Any idea? Do you even care?"

"Abby." Brian's voice was a low warning.

"Do you know that the death toll is going to be more than five thousand? More than *five thousand* people, five thousand Americans were just senselessly killed, burned alive by explosions and airplane fuel, crushed by concrete and steel, splattered on the pavement of Manhattan. *Five thousand people!*" She scoffed. "And you want to know what we want for dinner. Unbelievable."

In one quick motion, she rolled to her feet and left the room, her footsteps thumping down the basement stairs a few seconds later. In the silence that followed, Erica swallowed hard; embarrassed, hurt, and speechless. She couldn't remember ever having been bitch-slapped like that—and in front of other people. She felt humiliated. Tears pooled in her eyes.

Michael stood up. "Christ. I'm sorry, Erica. We should have all stopped watching this dreck hours ago. Details are continually being unearthed and it's just horrifying stuff, really. It's made us all so angry—even those of us who aren't American." His expression was gentle. "Abby's been having a rough day as it is and I'm afraid you just got the brunt of it." He approached her and held out his hand. "Come on, love. I'll help you with dinner."

They worked in companionable silence for a while, slicing and chopping. Erica got the water boiling and the tomato sauce simmering for the spaghetti while Michael prepared salads. Once Erica had given herself the time to calm down, she spoke.

"Wow," she said quietly, not wanting Abby to overhear her.

"I don't think she's angry with you, love. I think she's just angry." He stopped chopping celery and looked up, seeming to collect his thoughts. "I think it's hard to be Abby. I think she has this rosy view of the world, this sense that life is fair and people are good, and she's been trying to maintain that view even in the wake of what's happened. She's kept smiling, kept being cheerful, even though her mother and friends have been drastically affected, could have been killed. She's managed to hold tightly to her world view. But today, all those news reports, the playing of the video over and over and over." He shook his head. "I just think her innocence has been shattered."

Erica nodded, everything Michael said making sense. "You're probably right."

Her tone must have conveyed her hurt because Michael gave her shoulder a gentle squeeze. "Really, Erica, don't take it personally. She's probably down there right now feeling terrible about taking her frustrations out on you."

"Maybe."

"You were smart not to hang around here all day with us and watch that bloody telly. Horrible, horrible stuff, but like a train wreck: I couldn't manage to pull myself away. Now I can't get some of those images out of my head."

"I hear you," Brian said, scrubbing a hand over his face as he entered the kitchen. "Jesus. I've watched the replay a zillion times today and I still can't believe it's happened. It's almost surreal."

They set the table as a team, like they'd been sharing meals together for years. They set a place for Abby, even though all three of them knew she wouldn't be joining them. "I'll save her a plate," Erica said aloud to nobody in particular.

"Hey, did you say some flights are leaving?" Brian poked his fork in Erica's direction as they ate.

"That's what Corinne told me. The flights that came from Europe, some of them have been cleared to go back."

"But what if your destination wasn't Europe?" Michael asked. "Like me. I'm headed for Texas."

Erica shook her head. "I don't know the details. I mean, we all came from Europe, right? Our flight hasn't been cleared to go back. I wonder if it's the foreign airlines." She explained the story of the Lufthansa flight.

"That could be the case," Brian said. "American airspace is probably still closed, but European flights on European planes can't be held here indefinitely."

"Right." Michael sopped up his sauce with a slice of bread. "We should ask Tim when he gets back. He might know more."

"Seriously, how much longer can they keep us all stranded like this?" Brian asked. "I mean, I understand the caution behind it, but come on."

"People at the Lions Club are looking frazzled," Erica said. "They're doing okay, but they're snapping at each other. They're tired. They're frustrated."

"We had no idea how lucky we got when Corinne and Tim asked us to stay here. Can you imagine still being on those damn cots in a giant room with a hundred and eighty other people? I don't know how we ended up being the blessed ones, but I'm going to send one big-ass gift when I get home."

"That's a great idea. What are you thinking of?" Erica asked.

"I have no fucking clue."

Laughter was good; it helped ease the tension of all that the guys had seen that day, as well as helping Erica to feel better about her row with Abby.

"First thing we need to do is replenish the wine supply here," Michael said, gesturing to the rapidly emptying wine rack with his eyes.

"We could do that tonight," Brian suggested. "Go to that little shop we hit the other day?"

"You guys go ahead," Erica said. "I'm beat. I'll clean up here while you're doing that."

"You sure?" Michael said. "We all ate. I hate for you to clean it up alone."

Erica touched his cheek fondly. "Michael, if you weren't married and I didn't like girls, we'd be a match made in heaven."

He blushed all the way to his receding hairline, took her hand, and placed a chaste kiss on the back of it. "We all need to exchange addresses, e-mail addresses, whatever. Soon, lest we forget."

"Absolutely," Brian agreed. "At the risk of sounding sappy, I don't want to lose touch with you guys. You know?"

The three of them looked at each other. Michael still held Erica's hand and she reached her free one out to Brian. "I know," she said softly.

"Me, too," Michael added with a nod.

After a moment, Erica broke the silence. "Okay. Go. Find wine. I've got this."

The guys took the keys to Corinne's car and headed off to do a wine run while Erica took her time cleaning up the dining room and kitchen. She made individual plates up for Tim, Corinne, and Abby, not knowing if the MacDougals planned on coming home that night or if Abby ever planned to eat again. She put them all in the fridge with notes and smiley faces, wondering absently who she'd become in the past four days; was she now the woman who drew smileys on all her notes? Dotted her i's with hearts? Her team back home would find that rather amusing.

She loaded the dishwasher, wiped down the counters, put away the remaining bread, and poured herself the last of the cabernet. She thought about sitting outside, but the evening had cooled down considerably and she decided staying in was better.

A glance at the basement door told her what she really needed to do, but she hesitated. A fight was not something she was up for. And if she was being honest, she didn't even care about an apology at the moment. Abby was having a rough time making sense of it all. Hell, they all were. But Erica was a smart girl and she could see how it would be difficult for Pollyanna to wrap her happy little brain around the idea of killing thousands of people just to make a point. It had to be a hard lesson.

Taking a deep breath and then blowing it out, Erica stood. "Okay. Here we go." She opened the basement door and headed down the steps.

The first thing that hit her when the room came into view was a vague sense memory of Abby curled up behind her, wrapping her in the safety of her arms. *Perfect. That's all I need right now.* She took a slug from her wine glass and continued down.

Abby was sitting on the loveseat, her head tilted back, her arm thrown over her eyes. Her knee was bouncing up and down, telling Erica she was trying to keep herself from exploding.

"Hey," Erica said quietly, sitting next to her. "I saved you a plate of spaghetti. It's in the fridge if you get hungry."

"I'm not."

"Okay."

They sat in silence for long moments. Erica was sure Abby had more to say and decided she'd wait her out, hard as that was. Her patience paid off eventually.

"Doesn't it bother you?" Abby asked finally, not removing her arm.

"Doesn't what bother me?"

Abby heaved an annoyed breath. "The price of gas per gallon. Jesus. The whole thing at home. The planes flying into buildings. The people dying. The horror of it all. Doesn't it bother you at least a little bit?"

Erica's eyes widened at the implication. "Of course it bothers me. Of *course* it does. How can you think it doesn't?"

Abby removed her arm then, sat up and looked Erica dead in the eye. "How can you be so cheerful and smiling, then? You've barely smiled the entire time we've been here and suddenly today, after nearly four days of being stranded and seeing the horror on TV, you're suddenly in a good mood?"

Erica pressed her lips together, trying hard to find a way to explain something to Abby that she could barely explain to herself. "I don't know how to put this into words," she began. "I just—the whole thing is horrible. Of course it's horrible. How could you even think I wouldn't agree with you on that? But there's something about being here, in Gander, around these people. I don't know how to explain it, but today when I was helping Corinne and the other volunteers—I don't know." She threw up the hand without the wine glass. "I felt like I was doing what I was supposed to be doing."

"So, it's about you, then, is it?"

Erica sighed, trying to keep a lid on the hurt and annoyance she felt over being so harshly judged for speaking truthfully. "Don't you think this might be what those terrorists want? For all of us to be acting just like you?"

Abby cocked her head. "Excuse me?"

"Don't you think they'd be very happy to see us all crushed and broken? Tearful and in pain? I'm not saying we're not—and I can't believe I'm actually saying this, but—don't you think a better way to show our strength is to help each other get through it all, be there to support one another through the awful times that are no doubt screeching head-on in our direction? Isn't *that* the American way? If you were a terrorist, wouldn't that piss you off? Seeing your intended victims picking up the pieces and carrying on, carrying *each other* if necessary?"

Who am I? Erica thought as soon as she finished talking. None of this sounded like her. She was not patriotic. She was not a help-your-neighbor kind of girl. She had no idea where in her heart or mind this stuff was coming from. But she liked the way it sounded. And what was more: she believed it. She believed it all.

Abby looked at her, held her gaze, seemed like she was absorbing everything Erica had said. Then abruptly, she stood.

"I need a shower." The bathroom door shutting signaled the end of the conversation.

"Okay," Erica drew out. She rubbed a hand over her face, worried about Abby, but not knowing what else to do. Feeling the pull of home, she rummaged around for her cell phone and called her parents.

Chapter 13

Abby didn't understand what was happening to her.

She was horrified by the things she'd seen on TV. She was confused by the feelings sloshing around inside her. She was appalled by her own behavior.

Thank god Corinne and Tim weren't around. She couldn't bear the thought of them thinking her rude or ungrateful. That was not who she was. Abby Hayes wasn't rude or cruel or snide or mean. She was happy. Cheerful. Helpful. Kind. All the things she hadn't been to Erica just now.

With a groan, she turned the water on and let it run, waiting for it to get hot. Maybe if she was lucky, she could scald some of the disorder out of her head. Gingerly stepping into the steaming shower, she muttered to herself that she never should have watched the news reports all day. She should have found a way to pull herself from the screen, to peel herself out of the living room, to escape. She should have joined Erica at the Lions Club. At least there she could have done something, occupied herself, been useful. Scrubbing the toilets with a toothbrush would have been better than the helplessness she felt every time she watched a replay of a plane hitting a Tower, saw a shot of somebody frantically searching for a loved one, or observed the bewilderment on the faces of the people of New York City. Utterly and completely useless; that's how she'd felt all day. Sickened and useless.

Abby's skin reddened immediately. The water was too hot, but she let it run nonetheless, let it sluice over her skin, and she welcomed the discomfort, the almost-pain. It was nothing compared to what some Americans were going through this week.

The country would never be the same again; she knew that instantly. It was only fitting that she feel pain, too, that she share it. Her thoughts turned to the Bakers and she was hit by a wave of guilt. She should have gone with Erica today. She should have sat with Mrs. Baker, should have made sure Mr. Baker was eating. They were going through hell right now. The not knowing must have been killing them inside, slowly but surely; and instead of offering her support, Abby had laid on the floor in front of the tube all day long.

"What is happening to me?" she said aloud.

Anger like this was new to her. Anger and confusion. She didn't like it. It made her feel uncertain, out of control. She didn't like that she'd snapped Erica's head off. Abby was embarrassed about that. It was so unlike her. She should be glad Erica was enjoying pitching in; that was a big step for her. She should have been proud of her newest friend, not jealous of her good mood. Not envious that she wasn't destroyed.

Her poor mother. Abby knew that her mom was putting on a brave front, a purposeful façade so that Abby wouldn't worry about her. But Abby was a pro at reading people, especially those she loved, and she could hear the slight quaver in her mother's voice, note the faintly lower octave. The odds of Michelle Hayes *not* knowing somebody who'd died in the towers were pretty slim, but she'd pretend for Abby's benefit, not realizing that fooling her daughter wasn't something she could pull off any longer.

The thought of her mom losing somebody in the crush of concrete and metal brought her back to all the ghastly images that had assaulted her that day, and she ended up right back where she began: depressed, angry, and so confused. All the horror. All the death. It felt like it was raining down on her and she couldn't stop the tears any longer. They forced her to her hands and knees on the tile floor of the shower, the hot water beating down onto her back, the combination of steam and tears clouding her vision. The harder she tried to keep her emotions inside, the more they churned to find a way out until she couldn't hold the sob in any more. It ripped out of her and she felt like it took part of her soul with it. Her hand over her eyes, she had no choice but to give in as the anguish poured out of her.

She didn't hear Erica knocking on the door, had no idea that she'd pushed into the bathroom until the shower curtain was opened.

"My god," Erica exclaimed, her voice laced with concern and worry. "Abby?" Abby barely registered the words over her own crying, but she knew Erica had stepped right into the shower; she sensed her closeness. The water stopped. "Hey. What are you doing?" Her question was gentle as she reached for the towel and draped it over Abby's heaving back, wrapping her in the soft terrycloth. Hands rubbed her back tenderly and only when Abby felt Erica's breath near her ear did she realize she was kneeling on the shower floor with her. "Shh, it's okay. It's going to be okay, Abby. It is."

Words weren't possible for Abby. She continued to cry and let Erica wrap her arms around her, rock her slowly.

"So much death," Abby managed after a long moment. Her voice was gravelly, rough. "All that pain."

"I know," Erica said softly. She continued to move her hand up and down, stroking Abby's back.

"I just, I can't understand. All those people."

"Here. Come on. Let's get you up off this wet floor." Erica helped her to stand and step out of the shower onto the small, soft throw rug. For the first time since her meltdown, Abby looked at her roommate as they faced each other and Erica held the towel around Abby. Erica had changed into her sleeping attire and was barefoot in the white tank top and blue-and-white-striped panties. She'd gotten wet, was almost wetter than Abby now, and the steam had had its way with her hair, left it hanging in damp copper waves that skimmed along her shoulders. The tank top clung to every curve and her nipples made themselves known beneath the wet cotton. *Stunningly beautiful* were the first words that appeared in Abby's head. *Stunningly beautiful.* She swallowed hard, forced her gaze up to meet Erica's. The blue eyes that were normally so icy had changed, and the things Abby saw in them now were completely different than what she'd grown used to seeing. There was no judgment, no warning to keep her distance. Instead, there was concern in them. Tenderness.

Arousal.

Abby focused on the pulse beating visibly in Erica's throat. She suddenly seemed so vital, so alive, the undisputed antithesis of everything Abby had seen that day, and Abby wanted nothing more than to touch her, to feel her, to take her in.

"You're wet," she stated, oblivious to the double entendre.

"Yeah."

"I need—" Abby's dark brows met above her nose as she searched for the right words. *I need a hug, I need to touch your skin, I need to fuck your brains out.* "I need—"

Erica's only response was to lick her bottom lip and not move away.

And Abby couldn't stop herself.

Erica's back hit the bathroom door with a slam as Abby pushed into her, using her slight height advantage to pin Erica between the door and her body.

The kiss wasn't gentle. It wasn't tender. It was raw and hungry and demanding and it took Erica by surprise for a second before she kissed Abby back. Hard. The towel fell to the floor in a soggy heap as Erica wound a fist into the hair at the back of Abby's head and held on. It was a clash of teeth, tongues, and heat as Abby did her best to absorb the essence of Erica, to feel the blood racing through her veins, to feel her heart pounding with arousal, to feel *life*.

This is what I need, Abby thought as she maneuvered them through the bathroom door and into the room, all the while keeping her mouth fastened to Erica's. Her lips were so damn soft, her mouth hot and wet. At the edge of the bed, Abby finally wrenched herself away long enough to slide her hands up Erica's sides and take the tank top with them, toss it to the floor.

"Jesus," she whispered as she bared Erica's torso to the air. She was breathtaking, all creamy smooth skin, heaving breasts, and pink nipples, her muscle tone much firmer than one would expect. She wasn't fragile by any stretch of the imagination. She was strong and solid and absolutely gorgeous.

A light sprinkling of freckles dusted her shoulders and Abby wanted to start there, but was feeling so primal she was afraid she might bite, might actually break skin. Erica didn't wait for a decision and instead, grabbed Abby's face with both hands and kissed her, making Abby's head swim with the taste of her tongue, the crush of her lips. That was the moment Abby realized that Erica wanted this, needed this, just as badly as she did.

She pulled back suddenly, forcefully freeing herself from Erica's grasp. Without giving her a chance to catch her breath, Abby reached out and pushed against Erica's shoulders, giving her a gentle shove that sent her tumbling back onto the bed with a gasp of surprise. Abby followed her, crawling up her body and holding her prisoner, pinning her with hands and mouth and hips.

Few words were spoken; they were unnecessary, the only sounds filling the basement were groans, moans, and ragged breathing. The battle for control went on and on. Abby was taller, but Erica was stronger and each of them used her assets to turn the tables on the other. Despite the playfulness of their scuffle for the top, a seriousness lay beneath the surface. Something raw and base and vital. Abby used her long limbs to pin Erica's hands over her head while she left her mark on one of those beautiful shoulders, not only a way to show she'd been there, but an attempt to advertise that Erica still had blood running through her veins, that her body was full of precious life. Nothing proved that to Abby more than when she worked her way down Erica's body, yanked the panties off, and buried her head between strong, smooth thighs. Life was centered there—tangy, salty and sweet on her tongue, with a hint of musk and something primitive, something natural. Abby couldn't get enough. She pushed her tongue in as far as she could, trying to drink up everything, to consume the very essence of Erica and take it into her own body, her own heart, to feel that life. She felt Erica's hands in her hair, gripping her tightly and giving subtle direction. Her ears registered Erica's pleasure, her soft whimpers, her quiet pleading. When Abby replaced her tongue with her fingers, pushed in and curled them slightly, Erica groaned out her name and tears filled Abby's eyes. Much as she wanted to pick up the pace and to send Erica tumbling over the edge, she wanted this moment to last. Forever, if that was possible. She slowed things way down—despite Erica's whispered protests—and held her teetering for several long moments before finally granting her release. The strangled cry she emitted as her body arched and she held Abby's head tightly against her center, was the most beautiful thing Abby had ever heard in her life.

Tired and sweating, they were far from finished, and they continued to explore each other's bodies well into the night. Stroking, tasting, pushing, they spent hours milking every ounce of pleasure from each other that they could. They took turns—sometimes willingly and sometimes by force—coaxing with hands, tongues, and whispered words, wanting the night to never end, wanting to stay twisted into each other until the end of time, wanting not to face the day, the world, the anguish of what had happened back home. And though it may not have been clear to them in the middle of it all, somewhere in the backs of their minds, they knew what they wanted, they knew exactly why they had ended up naked and tangled up in each other's bodies on someone else's bed in the basement of a small house in Gander, Newfoundland: they wanted, they *needed* to feel alive.

September 15, 2001
Saturday

Chapter 14

Warm.

That was the first thought registering in Erica's brain when she swam up from deep sleep and settled into a light doze. She was so perfectly warm, she wanted to stay there forever.

Sated.

That was the next. She felt completely, utterly satisfied, almost intoxicated—pleasantly so. Her limbs were heavy but comfortable and she snuggled more tightly into the soft body that held her.

Sore.

That came third and brought a mischievous half-grin to her lips. Her inner thighs were tender. Her lips were swollen and a little chapped. A slight but insistent ache radiated from between her legs. She absently wondered at the fact that general muscle soreness was an annoyance, but muscle soreness as a result of crazy-hot sex was a badge of honor. Life was funny that way.

Erica cracked her eyes open just a touch and squinted to see the clock. 3:47 a.m. She gave a little sound of pleasure at the early hour, ecstatic that she needn't budge from the cloud of comfort surrounding her.

Now that she'd taken stock of her own body, she concentrated on the one beneath her. Abby's.

She was on her back, cradling Erica against her side, her breathing the deep, even rhythm of somebody fully asleep. One arm was wrapped around Erica's body, holding her close. The other was flung to the side, Abby's hand relaxed. Erica studied it. Abby had beautiful hands, with long, deceptively delicate fingers. A flash of those hands on her body hit Erica so hard, a small gasp pushed from her lips. She closed her eyes again.

Those hands were much stronger than they looked and those hands had had their way with Erica in more ways than one. Shoving her to the bed, ripping her clothes from her body, pinning her down, pushing into her. Erica swallowed hard as sense memory increased her heart rate, just the simple recollection triggering her arousal all over again, leaving her uncomfortably wanting.

She had no choice. That's what she told herself and she slowly and softly trailed her fingers down Abby's torso, over her tummy, and stopped at the very edge of the coarse dark hair. It wasn't her fault. She had completely lost control of her faculties; she wasn't thinking clearly. Abby had done something to her. The past few days had done something to her. Hell, this place had done something to her. This was not her. This was not the Erica Ryan she was used to, that her family and colleagues were used to. She didn't do this type of thing. Jump into bed with an utter stranger? Have incredibly hot, no-holds-barred, uninhibited sex in the bedroom of somebody she'd never met? And then lie awake thinking about when she could have more? No, that was not her. She had no idea who that was, but it was most definitely not her.

The heat from Abby's center still radiated and Erica could feel it against her skin. As she mentally counted all the ways she'd shocked herself over the past six or eight hours, her fingers seemed to act all on their own, traveling gently lower, to find Abby still wet and swollen. Exploration occurred all on its own, Erica alerted only when Abby's breathing changed. As if shocked, Erica's gaze jerked down to her hand, then up to Abby's face.

Blue eyes captured hers.

"I, I'm sorry," Erica stuttered, pulling her hand away. But Abby caught her by the wrist and held her hand in place.

"Don't be," Abby whispered. "And don't stop."

Something about the hoarseness of Abby's whisper and the solid grip she had on Erica's wrist made something inside Erica shift. The trepidation of three seconds before suddenly vanished and all at once she felt powerful. Dominant.

Alive.

She lifted her body slightly so she was positioned more above Abby, hovering, looking down at her. With one leg, she pulled Abby's to the side to give herself better access. Her touch no longer tentative, she rubbed her fingers through Abby's wetness, eliciting a gasp as she set up a rhythm. Abby's eyes drifted shut. Erica stopped all movement until they opened again.

"Keep your eyes open," Erica commanded. "Look at me." She didn't stop to wonder at her own bossiness, at how unlike her it was to tell her partner how to respond to her. All she knew was that for the first time in her life, the only thing she wanted to do was what felt right at that moment. And nothing in months had felt as incredibly, undeniably right as making love to Abby. Years, maybe. Right now, she didn't want Abby thinking about anything but her touch. No airplanes. No terrorists. No crumbling skyscrapers. No sorrow or anguish or death. Nothing but the two of them and the energy that swirled between them and the strange, wonderful connection they'd discovered.

"Erica?" Abby's voice was uncertain, her eyes questioning as they moved together.

"It's okay," Erica whispered, her eyes never leaving Abby's. "I've got you and it's okay. I promise. Do you trust me?"

Abby nodded, her breath becoming more ragged as their bodies began to rock as one.

"Good." The word was a feather-light breath against Abby's lips before Erica's mouth took them in a bruising, passionate kiss that ratcheted up the heat in the bed by several degrees. Erica picked up the pace, pushing inside Abby's body and nearly crying out at the hot flesh that surrounded her fingers. A few short moments after that, Abby wrenched their mouths apart and crushed the pillow over her face as the orgasm ripped through her, tearing a sound from her throat that began as a cry of ecstasy and turned into a wrenching sob of grief.

Erica was unsurprised, and she wrapped Abby up in her arms, murmuring to her, pressing tender kisses to her temple, her forehead, Erica's own eyes welling. "Shh. It's okay, Abby. I've got you. I'm right here."

Abby burrowed her face into the crook of Erica's neck and let it all out. All the sorrow and pain she'd felt over what she'd seen. All the agony and the torment. All the distress. All the suffering. She cried it all out against Erica's skin and Erica did exactly what was needed: she held her, she stroked her hair, she whispered words of gentleness and love. And after long moments, Abby's sobs receded and then finally tapered off until they were nothing but quiet hiccups.

Erica never let go, kept Abby wrapped up tightly in her arms, wanting her to feel protected from the world. People like Abby deserved to be protected from the world.

Eventually, sleep claimed them.

03 03 03

"Hey, you guys!"

Brian's voice boomed down the steps mere nanoseconds before he followed it, bounding like a ten-year-old, louder and more obnoxiously than necessary.

Abby jerked awake, blinking and confused, but immediately glad the sheet was covering anything important with regard to her very naked body. Next to her, however, Erica lay on her stomach, one arm thrown over Abby's torso and her entire back exposed, the sheet just barely covering her ass.

"Oh, for Christ's sake," she muttered, pulling the pillow over her head and grappling for the sheet. "Please tell me this is not happening."

Brian stopped at the bottom of the stairs and took in the picture before him, a devilish grin on his face. Abby couldn't help but smile, thinking he'd make the perfect big brother she'd always wanted.

"Much as I'd like to stand here for a minute—or an hour— and feast my eyes, and don't think I'm not filing this amazingly sexy picture away for future use, but I have more important news than the two of you knocking boots. Which I totally predicted, by the way, and Michael owes me ten bucks."

144

Abby made a rolling, hurry-up gesture with her hand. "What's the news?"

"We're going home!"

"What?" Erica pulled her head from beneath the pillow to make sure she'd heard correctly.

"We've been cleared, baby. We're supposed to get our things together and report to the Lions Club ASAP so we can be shuttled to the airport. We're going home!" He turned and took two steps at a time. At the landing, he looked over his shoulder and ducked so he could see the bed. He waved a finger in a circle to include both of them. "Incidentally, this? Fantasy material for years. *Years!*" He laughed evilly and went on his way.

Abby shook her head with a chuckle. When she turned, Erica was looking at her, a tentative smile on her face.

"Ready to go home?" Abby asked quietly.

Erica nodded. Inside, though, she wondered. Was she?

○३ ○३ ○३

It was hard to do something ASAP when really you wanted to do it as slowly as possible and make time come to a grinding halt. Erica had no idea why she was dragging her feet, but that's exactly what she was doing as she and Abby took turns in the bathroom and then packed what little they had with them. Erica touched Abby any chance she got, just simple strokes as they passed each other or tried to scoot around each other in the bathroom, trying hard to maintain the connection, but the closeness they'd shared not two hours earlier seemed to have vanished from Abby's memory. She whistled an off-key little tune as she gathered her things, smiling and happy and looking, in Erica's opinion, no different than she'd been the previous morning.

Erica felt like Abby hadn't been at all affected by their night together and she had a hard time swallowing that. Mostly because she had been very affected.

She wanted to broach the subject, wanted to talk about it, about all of it, but the words stuck in her throat and all she could manage was a weird grimace. She tried to focus on her bags, tried to concentrate on the fact that she was going to be going home, tried to think about the impending plane ride and what she should be wearing, and what the hell she was going to do once she got back to her condo in Raleigh. How could she possibly go back to her old life when she no longer felt like her old self? Was it even possible?

Abby continued to whistle and when she was finished with that, she hummed.

"Not a whole lot of packing to do, huh?" she said with a half-grin.

Erica simply blinked at her while Abby went back to what she was doing.

"I'm going to group all the stuff we brought here from the Lions Club—the shampoo and soap and stuff—and leave it for Corinne. Okay? I can't fit any of it in my backpack and you sure as hell don't have room in your laptop bag."

"Fine." It was the only word Erica could manage and it came out a bit more snappish than she'd intended.

"You okay?" Abby asked, her brow furrowed.

"I'm fine," she said again. *Stunning use of the English language, Ryan,* Erica thought. *Way to mix it up.*

Abby rolled her lips in and bit down, obviously wondering if she should inquire further. She didn't have to make that decision, though, because Erica couldn't hold it in any longer.

"Was I the only one here last night? This morning?" she asked, holding her arms out to her sides.

Abby's eyebrows met above her nose. "What?"

"I'm just wondering because right now, it feels like I was."

Abby took two steps toward her, reached out and rubbed her upper arm. "I was here," she said softly.

"I thought," Erica stumbled, fumbling for the right words. "I had—"

"Shhh." Abby tucked Erica's hair behind her ear, stroked a thumb over her cheek. "It was incredible. It really was."

Erica waited for more, searched Abby's blue eyes in anticipation, but nothing else came. Abby offered no more than a gentle smile. "That's it? 'It was incredible?' That's all you've got?"

Eyes widening, Abby asked, "What do you mean?"

Erica brushed Abby's hand away with a sarcastic bark of a laugh. "I should have known. Jesus, I'm an idiot."

"What are you talking about?" Abby asked and she sounded honestly flummoxed. Realization hit not long after that. "Wait, did you think? Oh."

Erica scoffed and shook her head slowly back and forth. "I'm not that naïve, Abby. I'm a big girl. I didn't think we'd get married. But I thought, I thought what happened last night—and this morning—was kind of special and that it might have meant more to you than your average one-night stand."

Abby chose her words carefully, Erica could see it on her face. "Last night was—" She shook her head, a wistful smile playing along her lips. "It was amazing. It was wonderful. I think it was just what we needed."

Erica flinched and then blinked rapidly. "Just what we needed?" Her voice was barely above a whisper.

"Yeah. Don't you think it was good for us? I do. I think it was good for you, especially." Abby's face held no malice, she was giving her own very general explanation of things and it drove Erica a little nuts.

"It was good for me especially." She stated it flatly, having no idea what to do with the sentence.

"You just, you cut loose." Abby used her hands for emphasis as her excitement seemed to increase. "You're so—forgive the word, but—you can be a little uptight. A little rigid. Everything in its place and all that. But last night, you went for it. You lived in the moment and experienced life. You were carefree. I bet it felt good."

Erica wanted to scream. And then she wanted to cry. How could she be so stupid? She hadn't expected some kind of declaration of love; she wasn't that childlike and ridiculous. But at the very least, she'd expected—what? She fumbled around in her brain for the right word, but got nowhere, which pissed her off further. The morning had started off so promising and now it was just a disaster. She did the only thing she knew how to do in this type of situation: she lashed out.

"Carefree? *Carefree?* Really? Is that what *you* are? All the traveling—which is really just running, let's be honest here. Your disdain for staying in one place too long. You think that's being carefree? Guess what, Abby: It's not. The correct word for what you are is care-*less*. Oh, you play at being Little Miss Sunshine, Little Miss Friends with Everybody, but the truth is, when it comes right down to it, you don't care about anybody but yourself." She was horrified to feel tears well up in her eyes and all she wanted was escape. Her voice cracked as she grabbed her stuff and said, "You're care-*less*."

She was up the stairs in an instant and Abby was left standing alone in the middle of the basement bedroom, wondering what, exactly, had just happened. Worse, she couldn't shake the image of Erica's beautiful face crumpled in pain or the tears brimming in eyes that had held hers so tenderly less than two hours before.

Chapter 15

It had barely been four days. Barely ninety-six hours since their flights had been diverted and just under seven thousand people invaded the tiny town of Gander. Less than a full week. Not even an entire work week, and yet somehow many of the Plane People felt closer to those they'd met in Gander than they did to some of their own family. So many emotions swirled in the atmosphere that morning, but the most common was the difficult combination of excitement to be going home, and sadness over having to say farewell to people who had come to mean so much.

The Lions Club was abuzz with the energized chatter of those about to head home. As three buses pulled into the parking lot and prepared to take them to the airport, the sound got louder, climbing from a gentle chittering to a loud and steady hum. Children ran around like they were hopped up on sugar; parents looked exhausted and yet happy; the elderly looked somewhat haggard, but relieved. Most people had been presented with opportunities at some point during their stay to wash up or even to shower, but many still wore the clothes in which they landed. They looked like a culture of people who had yet to be introduced to an iron.

Residents of Gander other than the MacDougals were making the rounds from place to place, helping the Plane People gather their things, to make sure nobody forgot anything. Hugs were commonplace, as were tears.

"Please be sure to check on, under, and around your cots," one tall man was saying loudly. "I know you didn't arrive with much, but make sure you're not leaving anything behind. I don't think you're going to want to come back any time soon." Many snickered at the joke.

Erica didn't have a lot to say. She was ecstatic to go home, was almost giddy knowing she'd be sleeping in her own bed that night. She wanted nothing more than to be smiling and celebrating with the other passengers on her flight, to show Abby that the previous night had meant as little to her as it had to Abby. Unfortunately, she was at a loss. Instead, she stood quietly and watched those around her, her laptop bag over one shoulder and a small, cheap tote bag she'd been given at the Lions Club that morning to carry the remaining items she'd purchased during her stay. She wore—once again—the work-out pants and T-shirt she'd bought at Walmart, and she suddenly felt so tired that, for the first time in years, she didn't give a crap what anybody thought about her appearance. She just wanted this all to be over so she could try to shoehorn herself back into her life.

She had no idea how.

Michael and Brian stood to Erica's right, talking animatedly with each other and with Abby, who was farthest to the right. Erica had purposely positioned herself as far away from Abby as possible, just as she had done in the car ride over and while they waited to board the bus. She didn't want to be close to her, to hear her laughter or get caught in the steady gaze of those blue eyes. She certainly didn't want to smell her, to have that unique combination of musk and baby powder assault her nostrils and remind her of the previous night.

Or that morning.

Erica closed her eyes and tried to force down the lump that had become ever-present in her throat.

When she opened them, Corinne and Tim MacDougal were standing in front of their foursome, their expressions both happy and sad at the same time. Erica was stunned to feel her own throat close up yet again and tears welled in her eyes.

Hands were shaken and slaps on the back occurred between the men as Corinne hugged Abby tightly and whispered something to her. Erica saw Abby's throat work as she swallowed and a tear spilled over and down her cheek. There was a lot of noise in the building at that point and Erica read Abby's lips rather than hear her thank

Corinne. Before she could take in any more, she found herself engulfed in Tim's arms. A quick squeeze and a whispered, "You take care of yourself, honey," and he was gone, wiping at his eyes as he left. Erica smiled after him, hugely touched, and knew her own tears were about to escape her eyes and course down her cheeks.

Corinne stood in front of her.

The emotion that enveloped her astounded Erica. She was not an emotional person and had worked hard to keep it that way. But this woman who stood in front of her now represented everything Erica thought of as loving and right and kind and good in the world, and there was no way to remain unaffected by that. Her heart clenched as Corinne wrapped her up in a loving hug. Erica tried her best not to burst into sobs.

"Thank you, Corinne," she whispered against an ear. "What you did for us, for all of us. You and Tim are incredible people. I can't begin to thank you enough."

"Nonsense," Corinne said, her voice cracking. "We did what anybody would do." She ended the hug and held Erica by her shoulders, fingers gripping tightly. She looked her directly in the eye. In a heated whisper, she ordered, "Don't hold on so tight. Everything's going to be fine, just trust in that. You don't have to hold on so tight." She hugged her again and then followed her husband's path away.

Erica's gaze followed her as she wondered about her words. When she looked at her three roommates, everybody's face was wet and each of them looked just a little bit heartbroken.

"Aren't we supposed to be happy to be on our way?" Brian asked in a surprisingly small voice. "To be going home?"

Michael, Erica, and Abby each nodded slowly, all eyes on Corinne as she walked away.

"Then why am I crushed?"

Nobody answered him because all felt the same way.

ଓ ଓଃ ଓ

On the bus ride to the airport, Abby sat with Brian, a good half-dozen rows behind Erica and Michael. Erica had hung back, obviously trying to put as much distance between herself and Abby. She heaved out a breath and looked out the window at the Canadian landscape that zipped by.

"So, you want to talk about what happened?" Brian asked.

"What happened when?" Abby knew Brian wasn't buying her playing dumb act, but she played it anyway.

"Between you and the hot redhead you were naked with this morning. You're sitting a mile-and-a-half away from her now, just a couple hours later."

"I don't know what happened." She felt Brian's eyes on her and she tried to ignore them, but finally had to give in. When she faced him, his expression shouted "skeptical." "What?" she asked, more heatedly than she'd intended.

"I can be a pretty gullible guy," Brian told her. "I know this. And I believe a lot of stupid things. But you know something I don't believe?"

Abby raised an eyebrow in expectation.

"I don't believe that you don't know what happened."

Abby groaned like a teenager, annoyed to be read so easily.

"Come on," Brian coaxed, wiggling his fingers in a give-it-to-me motion. "Tell Uncle Brian all about it."

With a defeated sigh, Abby launched into the story. Her intention was to edit heavily, to censor the personal stuff, but Brian's face was so open and his expression so concerned, she wished not for the first time that he was her big brother.

She told him everything.

From her meltdown in the shower to her post-coital blubbering in Erica's arms and everything in between, astonishing even herself with her own honesty. She told him about the gentle look on Erica's face, as well as the panic it instilled in her.

"So, you blew her off?" Brian asked, no accusation in his tone.

"I didn't blow her off," Abby responded testily. "I just, she took me by surprise. That's all."

"You know, I seem to recall you getting all kinds of self-righteous and giving me crap when I suggested you 'tap that.'" He made air quotes. "You told me that was the big difference between men and women. So, looks like you're one of us, baby. Congratulations."

It sounded to Abby like he was only half-kidding and she wanted to defend herself, but any explanation died in her throat before it ever reached her lips.

"What are you afraid of?" he asked, quietly now. "She didn't propose marriage, did she?"

"No."

"Did she ask you to move to—where does she live, North Carolina? Did she ask you to move there?"

"No."

"Then what? What scared you so much?"

So many thoughts swirled through Abby's head in that moment that she had to blink rapidly to hold on to her equilibrium. *She looked me in the eye while we were in bed. She didn't laugh at my tears. She took the brunt of my anger and never struck back at me. She held me when I fell apart. She made love to me.* There had been very few women in her life about which she could say any *one* of those things, let alone *all* of them.

That was what scared her so much, but try as she might, she couldn't bring herself to say it out loud. Instead, she shrugged like she was fifteen again. "I don't know."

Brian's quiet scoff told Abby he wasn't buying it, but she just looked out the window.

Several rows up, Michael and Erica sat together amidst the hum of the rest of the excited passengers.

"You all right, love?" Michael asked, gently bumping Erica with his shoulder.

She offered him a half-grin. He'd found time to have the business suit he was wearing on Tuesday dry-cleaned and pressed, and he looked fresh and dapper. She felt a surge of affection for him and reached over to straighten his striped tie. "Yeah. I'm good. You?"

He seemed to think about that carefully, as if choosing and discarding various thoughts before settling on one in particular. "Do you feel different?"

Erica cocked her head to one side. "Different? What do you mean?"

"I mean do you feel that this whole experience has changed you? In some way?"

"Absolutely." She was surprised she answered so honestly so fast, but it was true. "I don't know how to describe it. I can't define it. The only thing I know for sure is, something's changed in me."

Michael nodded. "That's it exactly."

They were quiet for the rest of the ride, each absorbing what the other had said, wishing they had something more concrete to illustrate what they were feeling, but at the same time, relieved that they weren't the only one.

ର ଔ ର

By the time the plane was full and everybody had taken their seats, things had quieted only slightly, going from an excited chatter to a gentler, calmer hum. Facial expressions were all over the place. Most passengers were ecstatically happy. Giddy even. Others were more serene, uncertain about what would happen next. And some faces were etched with worry and fear, wanting terribly to get to their destinations, but afraid of what might await them there.

The Bakers fell into that last category.

Abby knew there was nothing she could do or say to make them feel any better, but that didn't stop her from trying.

She knelt backward in her seat, as she had on the flight in, and did her best to reassure and comfort the Bakers. As of their last conversation with their daughter—which took place just before they'd left the Lions Club—there was still no word on Tyson, and his parents looked crushed by their worry, as if it was a physical weight pushing down on their shoulders and stooping their spines. Other members of their family had been posting flyers with Tyson's picture, asking for information from anybody who might have seen him. It was all they could do. Abby couldn't begin to imagine what they were going through—the not knowing, the constant wondering. She patted Mrs. Baker's hand like she was an elderly woman and made appropriate sounds—and felt unequivocally helpless.

Jeffrey the flight attendant clicked on the PA. "Good morning, ladies and gentlemen. We're happy to report we'll be on our way shortly, so if you all would take your seats and fasten your seat belts, we'd appreciate it." Excitement colored his voice and only then did it occur to Abby that the flight crews—all thirty-nine of them—had been stranded just like the rest of them.

As she gave Mrs. Baker's shoulder a final squeeze and shifted her position in her seat, Abby was caught by icy blue eyes. Erica held her gaze and didn't look away and Abby had a sizzling flash of that same gaze holding hers as long fingers filled her, stroked in and out, coaxed her into oblivion. She swallowed down the lump in her throat and gave what she hoped was a small smile, then sat forward and fastened her seat belt with trembling hands while releasing an unsteady breath.

Half a dozen rows up, she could see Brian and Michael sitting directly across the aisle from each other. She couldn't hear what they were saying, but she wondered how they were feeling at that moment, what they were thinking. Did Michael have his mind back on work already? Did he feel like he'd fallen behind by losing four weekdays? Did Brian even want to go home? Was he ready to return to his life as a newly divorced man?

Abby had been too wrapped up in her own shit with Erica to bother asking.

You're careless.

Erica's words bit at her.

You don't care about anybody but yourself.

Was she right?

Abby spent the rest of the flight trying *not* to focus on that question. After all, it wasn't true. She wasn't selfish. She was a good person. Brian had asked what she was afraid of. Abby scoffed, causing the gentleman next to her to look up from his Tom Clancy novel with expectantly raised brows.

155

"I'm not *afraid* of anything," she said to him, determined.

"Oh. Um, okay. Great. Good for you." He went back to his book.

ଊ ଊ ଊ

The slightly balding man in the window seat whom Erica had dubbed the Snoring Man had a real name: Bob. Erica found, much to her surprise, that talking to him wasn't something she wanted to avoid. On the contrary, she introduced herself and started up a conversation.

"Can you believe we're finally going home?" she asked him as they taxied down the runway. "I was beginning to wonder if we'd be stranded here forever to wear the same three outfits over and over until the end of time."

Bob chuckled. "I almost crapped myself when they said we couldn't have our baggage. I've got blood pressure meds and my shaving stuff and half my life in that suitcase."

Takeoff was smooth and both of them gazed wistfully out the window as Gander and Canada receded.

"Such an amazing place," Bob said quietly, almost to himself. "I still can't believe it."

"I know what you mean."

He turned to her and his eyes were intense. "Seriously. I can't believe it. The pharmacy got me my meds free of charge. And then the cashier invited me and the five people in line behind me to her house for showers and dinner. We ended up crashing all over her furniture for three nights. She wouldn't let us do a thing and she fed us like royalty."

Erica told him about the MacDougals and how incredible they'd been, how well they'd taken care of the four of them. "I don't even know when they slept," she said, her voice filled with awe.

"I've heard a lot of stories like this," Bob told her.

"The people we stayed with lent us their car."

"How crazy is that?" Bob asked with a laugh. He shook his

156

head, bewildered, and rubbed at his ear. "I like to think I'd have been as generous if the roles were reversed, but I'm not sure. And I'm embarrassed to say that."

"I know exactly what you mean. I've been—I don't know what the right word is—touched? softened? changed?—by this whole thing. It's been one of the most bizarre experiences of my life."

"In a good way?"

"In a good way. Despite what happened at home, yes, in a very good way."

"For me, too. I don't think I'm the same person anymore."

They smiled at each other, sharing something indefinable. Bob didn't think he was the same person anymore. That was as good a definition as any that Erica had tried to come up with. Abby's words came back to her.

You're so—forgive the word, but—you're a little uptight. A little rigid. Everything in its place and all that. But last night, you went for it. You lived in the moment and experienced life. You were carefree. I bet it felt good.

At the time, those words had stung in a nasty, painful way; but weren't they true? Hadn't Abby simply been stating facts? Erica *had* gone for it. She *had* lived in the moment. And it *had* felt good.

Erica wondered if others on the plane were feeling similar emotions. As she looked around, she could swear the atmosphere felt different somehow. Charged. True, most people were almost visibly vibrating with the anticipation of finally being on their way, but there was something else. She suspected she might never be able to put a finger on it, to define it in some tangible way; but to break it down into its simplest form, she liked the way she felt.

She *liked* the way she felt.

She hadn't thought such a thing in a long, long time.

Chapter 16

Erica had lost track of time. She had no idea how long the flight was. Which time zone she was in was a mystery to her. What she did know was that Bob was a widow who was on his way back from visiting his first grandchild, a boy named Cameron, who was born a month before. His daughter and son-in-law lived in London and Bob puffed up like a peacock when he talked about his grandson. He had his camera with him and showed pictures of a tiny little infant with a shock of black hair. Erica was engrossed, ooo-ing and ahh-ing over the itty-bitty fingers and toes.

To Erica's right sat Joan and Sylvia, two sisters in their sixties who'd taken a vacation to Ireland, something they'd been planning for over a decade. They laughed and blushed and regaled Erica and Bob with stories of all the shopping they'd done (having to purchase an extra suitcase in order to fly their purchases home) and the many pubs they'd visited.

It eventually occurred to Erica that her behavior on the plane ride to New York was the complete opposite of how it would have been just five days ago. She absently wondered if she should start labeling her life in terms of B.G. and A.G.—before and after Gander. B.G., she would have kept to herself on the plane. She would have made it very clear to those around her that she was not interested in conversation, that she did not care where anybody else was going, and that she had no intention of sharing where she was going. Headphones were very good for making this point and she vaguely remembered that she had a small set in her laptop case, but made no move to get them. Now there was nothing she wanted to do more than converse with the people around her, listen to their stories, and ask them questions. She shook her head in wonder. A.G. life was bizarre.

When the landing gear of the plane hit the pavement, bounced once, then settled into a loud, speeding roll, the entire crowd in the plane cheered. While nobody wanted to think about what had happened here—and while many of them were about to experience the aftermath—there was something about being on American soil, something about being on the soil of New York that had the passengers swelling with pride. Erica's eyes filled and when she glanced at Bob, his were wet as well. They both gave embarrassed chuckles.

"We're home," he said softly.

"Thank god," Erica replied, and sniffed.

Deplaning was more difficult than most people expected and it crossed Erica's mind that such might be the case on every plane that had been stranded in Gander. Each flight's passengers had been accommodated together in Canada (at first, at least), so each manifest contained a list of people who were bonded, tied together forever by the people of a generous town. E-mail addresses were exchanged. Phone numbers were recited and written down. Street addresses were given. Though anxious to be on their way, few found it easy to get off the plane and go.

They lingered in their seats, in the aisle. They meandered down the walkways and loitered around the gate. They moseyed through Customs. They dawdled at the baggage claim even though many of them had connecting flights or no baggage to grab. Erica exchanged e-mail addresses with Bob and promised to keep an eye out for more pictures of Cameron. Joan and Sylvia vowed to send her the names of the best Irish whiskey they'd had so she could pass the name on to her friend at work, who loved any and all whiskey. She hugged all three of them tightly and promises to keep in touch were spoken one last time.

The tug at her heart surprised her as she watched them walk off in different directions.

When she turned back to the crowd, she looked right into Brian's sparkling green eyes. Michael and Abby stood nearby.

"You weren't going to leave without saying goodbye, were you?" he asked with a wink.

"Of course not," she said truthfully.

"I don't know about the rest of you, but I'd like contact information for all three of you," Michael said, pulling a small notebook from the inside pocket of his suit coat. "I feel like you're all part of my family now." He shrugged as if saying he had no explanation for it, it just was.

Abby reached into her backpack. "I've got some paper, too." She looked tired, Erica thought, but her eyes were still beautiful and her skin was still creamy and her disheveled dark hair only made Erica want to reach out and brush it back. She let out a quiet breath instead.

Information all exchanged, the four of them stood looking from one face to another, nobody wanting to be the first to leave. After a few moments, they all laughed and Brian spoke up.

"I have a connecting flight to catch, as do you two, I think." He nodded at Erica and Michael. "And I've had more than enough good-bye in my life recently, so I'm not going to say it to you guys. Instead—" His voice cracked and he glanced down at his shoes as his eyes welled, then his cheeks flushed. "Jesus, look at me." Erica touched his shoulder as Abby rubbed the opposite arm. He steadied himself. "Instead, I'm going to say thank you for keeping me sane over the past four days. I'm going to say that I love you all, and I'm going to say I'll catch you later."

He reached a hand out to Michael, who took it and pulled him into a heartfelt hug.

"Take care, man," Brian said, his voice muffled against Michael's shoulder.

"You, too."

Erica was next. She tried to keep herself together, but then wondered why. A single tear spilled over and down her cheek. "You take care of yourself, gorgeous," he ordered her.

"You do the same," she said back, her throat threatening to close on her.

He didn't even look at Abby; he simply turned and she was in his arms. Erica watched as they held each other, whispering, squeezing. When they parted, Brian sniffled, shifted his bag on his shoulder, and gave them one last smile.

"Catch you later."

They watched him disappear into the crowd.

"I can tell you for certain that I won't last if we drag this out," Michael said with a self-deprecating grin. He reached out for them and pulled them both into a group hug. "It was my honor to spend time with you two wonderful women. Please be good to yourselves and to each other. And if you're ever in London again—or Dallas, for that matter—you've got a place to stay and a friend with whom to dine. All right?"

Both women nodded against him, neither trusting themselves to speak, neither able to stop the free flow of tears now.

When they parted, his eyes were wet, too. He pushed a strand of Abby's hair behind her ear, then reached to stroke a tear from Erica's face with his thumb, as if he was comforting his daughters.

"Keep in touch."

Erica and Abby stood shoulder to shoulder as he walked away. Similar scenes were occurring all over the airport. The two of them looked around, seeing people hugging, crying, scribbling notes. Their gazes eventually met and held for long moments.

"And then there were two," Abby said. When Erica didn't reply, she began, "Erica, listen—"

"No. It's okay." Erica cut her off with an upheld hand. She'd rehearsed this in her head during the bus ride and again on the plane and during those rehearsals, she'd realized something that surprised her: it was true. "Look, you don't owe me anything. I don't owe you anything. The circumstances were certainly extenuating." She said the last line with a gentle laugh. "And we both enjoyed ourselves. You're right. It doesn't have to be more than that."

Abby blinked at her as if wondering when Erica had been body-snatched and replaced with a look-alike. Before she could say anything else at all, she was engulfed in Erica's arms.

They stood like that for what felt like hours, holding tightly to each other, each of them knowing that what they'd experienced

161

together went beyond even the bond that most of the Plane People felt with each other, and they didn't want to let go. But Erica had a connection to make and Abby needed to grab her bag and find her mother, so they eventually managed to separate.

"You're an amazing woman, Ms. Ryan," Abby whispered, toying with the ends of Erica's hair.

"You're not so bad yourself, Ms. Hayes," Erica responded as she looked up into those breathtaking eyes.

"I don't know what else to say. I feel like there's so much, but—" She shook her head. "It's probably too much, so I don't know what to say." Her tone was gentle and her expression was both apologetic and uncertain.

"Then don't say anything," Erica told her softly. "Just kiss me and we'll go. Okay?"

Abby stepped close. Erica inhaled, trying to take in the scent of her and sear it into her memory. Abby touched Erica's shoulder, slid her hand down her arm and entwined their fingers. Erica tipped her head up and when their lips met, suddenly there was nobody else. There was no bustling airport crowd. There were no announcements over the PA. There weren't people jostling them to get to the baggage carousel. There was only Erica and Abby and the sweet tenderness of their kiss.

They stepped back from each other a little breathless, separating yet keeping eye contact. Abby adjusted her backpack on her back; Erica hefted her laptop case on her shoulder and shifted her grip on the tote bag, each continuing to step backward as they did so. Finally, Erica lifted one hand and gave half a smile.

"Bye, Abby."

Abby returned the wave. "Bye."

Erica turned and headed toward her gate.

She tried to ignore the hot tears streaking her face.

She didn't look back.

October 15, 2001
Monday

Chapter 17

Exactly four weeks after departing Gander, Newfoundland, Abby had yet to leave Connecticut. She'd had plans to; she was going to stop in and visit with her mother, stay with her for two nights, then hop another plane and zip across the country to San Francisco. There was going to be partying and reminiscing with her friend Gina from high school. Then she was going to catch a bus and ride up the coast to Portland to visit her cousin, Derek.

All those plans fell away upon her return when her mother wrapped her in an embrace and began to cry. Abby felt like she was ten years old again and wanted nothing more than the safety and security of her mother's arms at that moment and for several days afterward. It was only during that hug, during that physical connection, that it occurred to her it was really just luck that had kept her mother—or her father or her uncle or any number of her friends—from being anywhere near Ground Zero on September eleventh. Anybody could have gotten caught in the horror. Anybody did.

Abby's parents were divorced, had been since Abby was ten. Her father had been traveling for work on the eleventh and had ended up stranded in Phoenix. He returned from *his* exile a day after she did and they met for dinner soon after. He was as emotional as her mother, without the tears. He looked at her, touched her, kept stroking her hair as if he was uncertain she was really there with him.

Friends called constantly, checking on one another. They got together much more often than normal. Abby heard from friends she'd lost touch with and instead of being suspicious, she was touched. She called her college roommate who lived in New Jersey, even though they hadn't spoken in almost a year. All the spontaneous contact was strange, but somehow comforting.

The attacks on the towers had changed the attitude of the entire country. A full month later and it was still first and foremost on the minds of the majority of the American population, especially those in and around New York City. The country had been sucker punched, and she was confused, angry, and devastated by the loss of over 3,000 of her people. New Yorkers who weren't enraged walked around in a zombie-like state, wandering and bewildered, some still posting flyers and searching for loved ones who had yet to be found, holding out hope that they weren't buried in the rubble of the towers, despite knowing that was the most likely place. Television news finally started to cover other stories, but there were still pieces running on the victims of the attacks. You didn't have to look hard to find nonstop reporting, and Ground Zero had become a hub of endless activity: debris being moved, shifted, rifled through; body parts being catalogued and—hopefully—identified.

Keeping in touch with the Bakers was hard, but important to Abby. In fact, she had been visiting them at their home in Brooklyn two-and-a-half weeks after their return from Newfoundland when the call came in that rescue workers had finally found and identified the body of Tyson Baker. By then, the entire Baker family had accepted that Tyson was probably lost to them, but the confirmation was devastating. Abby took her leave right away, reluctant to intrude upon a scene that should be limited to family. She'd managed to hold it together for most of the train ride home, but her shields crumbled quickly and she'd spent the rest of the day in her room, crying and heartbroken for a family that didn't deserve such pain.

And then her brain went on a rampage for the umpteenth time about how no family deserved such pain, and she was angry and upset about the situation all over again.

Such was the life of a New Yorker a mere month after the attacks.

It was exhausting and depressing and yet Abby couldn't bring herself to leave.

When she wasn't busy being upset or trying to comfort friends who'd lost family or family who'd lost friends, Abby's thoughts always returned to the same subject: Erica.

They hadn't spoken since the airport. They hadn't e-mailed. Abby had dialed the first six digits of Erica's cell phone on at least five occasions, but had never been able to follow through with the call. What would she say? How would she open? What could they talk about that wasn't the one night of incredibly passionate sex they'd had? Because that's what was most prominent in Abby's mind: the sight of Erica's naked body beneath her, the smell of her arousal, the sound of her climax. Sure, there were a lot of other things and she had the unfamiliar desire to learn more about the beautiful, sexy, quiet, confusing and moody woman with whom she'd shared a room for three nights, but the sex . . . *Jesus, the sex.* She couldn't get it out of her head. The connection they'd made was new to Abby, unfamiliar and impossible to ignore.

E-mails from both Michael and Brian had arrived on a fairly regular basis since they'd parted in the airport, the first from each coming within a day or two of Abby's return home. After that, every few days and no less often than once a week. Both men were doing fine, Michael back in England and Brian thinking of asking out a woman in the office building across the street from his. Abby wondered if either of them had been in contact with Erica, but felt weird asking because they'd know right away that she had *not* been and they'd want to know why. Well, Michael would want to know why. Brian would already know why and he'd get all over her about it. So she kept quiet.

Inexplicably restless on that Monday morning, Abby had two sharp thoughts hit her out of the blue. One: she had to *do something.* She had no desire to run off to the far reaches of the country again—she was surprisingly happy just being at home and close to her family—but she was feeling useless, like dead weight, and decided she'd laid around long enough. It had been a long time since she'd felt like she was contributing to society and, just like that, she knew that it was time to get back to it. She vowed to look into ways she could help. Right after she accomplished the other thing taking up too much space in her brain: the need to contact Erica.

She'd waited long enough. She'd been a coward long enough. She'd thought about Erica long enough. She'd missed her long enough.

Abby stopped and examined those thoughts. She'd missed Erica? Was that true?

There really was no question; she had. Admitting it to herself felt strangely liberating. *Yes, I've missed the woman I spent a whopping ninety-six hours with. So sue me.*

She rifled through some papers on the small computer desk in the corner of her mother's dining room and pulled out the one with contact information for Michael, Brian, and Erica. Then she stared at the telephone for a long while as she tried to formulate in her head exactly what she'd say. After twenty frustrating minutes, she muttered, "Fuck it," and dialed.

On the fourth ring, Abby glanced at the clock and realized it was mid-morning and Erica was probably at work, like most normal people. Still, her breath caught as Erica's calm, smoothly recorded voice came on the line.

"I can't come to the phone right now, but if you leave your name, number, and a brief message, I'll get back to you as soon as I can. Thanks."

The most generic of generic messages, but Abby still called back three more times to listen. Bits and pieces of things Erica had said during their short time together began firing through her head like race cars zipping past at exorbitant speeds.

". . . there's only one bed."

"You couldn't afford me."

"I'm going to hate myself in the morning. And you."

"Keep your eyes open. Look at me."

"Do you trust me?"

"It's okay, Abby. I've got you. I'm right here."

Abby didn't allow herself to let it go any further. She didn't want to recall Erica telling her how careless she was, how she didn't give a rat's ass about anybody but herself. Instead, she gave up on the phone and went to the computer. Maybe an e-mail was the better way to go.

But just as she had been stuck on what to say over the phone, she was equally puzzled by what to type in an e-mail. Should she keep it general, impersonal? *Hi, how are you? What's new?* Or should she dive right into the specific? *I can't stop thinking about you and I know it's weird, but I miss you.*

With a frustrated groan, she began typing. Then she backspaced so she could start over.

She typed a different sentence, then pounded on the backspace key some more, muttered curses escaping her lips.

"Why is this so difficult?" she asked aloud. "It's a goddamn e-mail. I just want to say hi, ask how she's doing. What's the big freaking deal?"

Finally, after taking many deep, steadying breaths, she settled down and did what her mother had always told her was the best way to write a letter. She wrote from her heart.

Hi, Erica

I apologize for not contacting you sooner than now, but I've been thinking a lot about you and I wanted to say hello. How are you? Have you settled back into work? Have you heard from Michael and Brian? Or the MacDougals? It's kind of weird that I could miss a place I only spent four days in—and under not-so-favorable circumstances—but I do. Do you ever feel like that?

Anyway, I hope you're well. I tried calling, but got no answer. I forgot you have a job. ☺ If you get a free minute, drop me a line and let me know how you're doing. I miss you.

Abby

She debated the "I miss you" for several long moments before deciding to leave it in. After all, whether Erica thought it was weird or not, it was the truth. Her finger hovering over the mouse button, which in turn kept the cursor hovering over the word "send," Abby wavered one last time before giving in and clicking.

It was off. There was no turning back, and she immediately began wondering what she'd do if Erica never responded. It would sting more deeply than she cared to admit, so she decided a distraction was in order. It was time to, as had crossed her mind earlier, *do something.*

Volunteering their time had always been something the members of the Hayes family were big on, even before Abby's parents split up. It had been important to them to teach their daughter the importance of giving her time, that it was her duty to give what she could to those less fortunate than she was. She'd done everything from work at a soup kitchen to ringing the bell for the Salvation Army's red kettle campaign. Volunteering was nothing new to Abby and it was something she enjoyed doing. Her mother had many different contacts, but Abby knew that in this situation, she should go right to the big guns: the American Red Cross. She made a call.

ભ ભ ભ

Dressing in layers to combat the chilly October morning that was due to become a fairly warm October afternoon, she left a note for her mother, stocked a backpack with snacks, her wallet, an extra pair of socks, and a baseball hat, and headed for the train into the city.

Riding the train—or the subway—was a way of life for people who lived in, lived around, or worked in New York City, and most of the time the landscape inside one of the cars was standard. People kept to themselves, reading books or newspapers, silently head-bobbing to the music from their earbuds, working on their laptops, quietly directing tourists at which stop they should disembark, napping. Abby had noticed a change, however, in the month since the attack on the towers. Passengers seemed more—dazed? Was that the right word? Bewildered? Many simply stared into space as if wondering where they were and how they'd gotten

170

there. Others showed angry expressions, scowled, eyebrows dipped to form a V above the bridge of their noses; Abby questioned if those people even knew they were doing it, if they could feel the divot, the slight squint. Anybody who even sort of resembled somebody who might possibly be of Middle Eastern descent often received looks of disdain, even of downright hatred. Of all the side effects of 9/11, that one broke Abby's heart. The terrorists had succeeded in taking a city known for its cultural diversity and making its people suspicious of that diversity.

The bustling of activity at Ground Zero seemed almost apropos, this being Manhattan. If the borough was anything, it was bustling. Even a month later, swarms of people were busy working. Digging, moving, helping in some way—in *any* way—to get things back to some semblance of normal.

Abby had no trouble finding the Red Cross trailer that served as indefinite headquarters, and within a half hour of her arrival she was helping to hand out water and snacks to the exhausted, dirt-covered workers, adding her own pats on the back and thank yous for all their time and effort. It was astonishing to watch, even a month after the attacks. The firefighters, EMTs, police, and K9 rescue units all working like a giant army of ants, everybody with a job to do, everybody with head down, diligently toiling to accomplish the task at hand. Some with smiles and attempts to lighten the mood just a bit, others with serious—often stricken—expressions, still horrified.

Hours later, Abby sat on a curb, nibbling a granola bar, her sweatshirt tied around her waist, a dark ponytail threaded out the back of her New York Mets ball cap, watching and amazed that the energy level hadn't seemed to drop even a little bit as the day went on. Hundreds upon hundreds of flyers showed faces of the missing and they all seemed to stare at Abby, plead to her. She'd actually seen one of Tyson Baker earlier, his dark eyes kind like his mother's, his white teeth gleaming inside his fabulous smile. She somehow managed not to burst into tears right there in the street—even though that's exactly what many people did.

"Hey, are you Abby?" The voice startled her. A tall young man

171

with sandy hair and a scruffy chin that made him look older than he probably was regarded her with gentle brown eyes.

"That's me."

"Hi. I'm John." He held out his hand and Abby shook it. "Roberta sent me to find you. We're running low on masks and gloves and she wants us to run over to that medical supply place. They have more for us."

Abby stood, ready to be moving again. "Lead the way."

John gestured for Abby to follow him.

The medical supply place was only a couple blocks away, so they hoofed it. John explained that the items they were to pick up would be on a rolling cart for easy transport, since traffic was still unpredictable and often clogged. The building housed pharmaceutical offices and laboratories according to the signage and the medical supply company was on the ground floor.

"Ugh," John said as he held the door for Abby. "Science hated me in school."

"Me, too. Chemistry might as well have been a foreign language."

"Right? I think I passed by the skin of my teeth."

A tall, lanky African-American man met them and gestured to two rolling carts like he was Vanna White showing off letters. They were loaded down with paper masks, boxes of gloves, plastic bags of plastic bags, paper towels, bottled water. John and Abby each took positions behind a cart.

"Shall we?" John asked as he pushed his cart forward and out the door the man held open.

Abby wanted to challenge him to a race, but managed to keep herself in check. "Right behind you," she said instead.

The wheels of the cart on the pavement made enough noise to prohibit conversation, so Abby's mind drifted as she walked. Despite the horror that had been spread over the city, it was still a melting pot. As she looked around the street, she saw people of all shapes and sizes. An older man with silver hair and glasses passed her on the left. A college-age woman with a thick blond braid and skin so pale it was almost translucent spoke firmly into her cell phone. An African-American woman gave her a half-smile as she passed. *Obviously a tourist,* Abby thought. Beyond that woman a flash of color caught Abby's eye, just a quick zip of copper that was then blocked by a number of people moving as a group on the other side of the street. Abby squinted and moved her head, trying as best she could to see around them.

"You coming?" John asked from several yards in front of her as he glanced back and saw her slow down.

"Yeah, I'm coming, but . . ." The crowd moved slowly, a mishmash of eight or nine people walking as if they were one entity, but finally somebody moved and Abby saw the copper again. It was a ponytail and it was the exact color of . . . no. That was impossible. Wasn't it? What were the odds? *Slim to none,* she told herself, shaking her head, but unable to look away as she walked. *Ridiculously slim to none.* Deciding she was being silly, Abby picked up her pace. At that exact moment, the woman turned and looked in her direction. Abby's heart stopped.

"Erica?" she said with disbelief as the woman met her gaze, and smiled widely.

That smile was the last thing Abby saw before she crashed her cart headlong—and very loudly—into a trash can and ended up on her ass, covered in garbage, medical supplies, and her own embarrassment.

173

Chapter 18

"No, it's okay. I've got this. She's a friend."

The familiar voice drifted into Abby's brain as she took mental stock of her body, making sure all the parts worked, that nothing had been broken, that everything was where it should be. When she was certain things were functional, she gradually looked up. Blue eyes that she'd always thought of as icy looked down at her, this time with warmth and genuine concern.

"Erica?" she croaked a second time, still not able to believe that's who it was.

"Hey. Nice dismount. Are you okay?" Erica stroked the hair off Abby's forehead with one hand, held on to her forearm with the other.

"I'm fine. Nothing bruised but my ego." Abby studied her, studied her face. Erica looked different somehow. Not physically—she was still the same stunningly beautiful woman Abby had shared the most poignant four days of her life with—but something in her eyes, in her face. Abby couldn't narrow it down and she squinted as she tried.

"What are you doing here?" It was the obvious question, so she asked it.

"Working," Erica said simply.

"But you work in North Carolina."

Erica picked various sundries off Abby's legs, handing them to John, who was restocking her cart with the items she'd dumped. Erica's warm hand still lay on Abby's arm. "Right. I do. That's where my company is based, but the company I work for sent several scientists here to help with the research and study of those anthrax letters."

"Oh my god," Abby gasped, thinking of the news reports she'd seen about envelopes of anthrax powder that had been mailed to various media outlets and a couple senators barely a week after the attacks. The government was working tirelessly to find answers, despite the chaos already affecting the country.

"It's okay," Erica reassured her.

"It's dangerous. Isn't it dangerous?"

"We're careful. It's okay."

"But . . ." Before she could say more, before she could find a way to express her anxiety, a young man from the group Erica had been a part of bent to her and said something in low tones.

Erica nodded. "Okay. I'll be right there." She looked at Abby with an apologetic half-smile. "Listen, Abby, I have to go. But—" Her voice trailed off as if she wasn't sure what to say.

"I e-mailed you," Abby blurted.

Shock zipped across Erica's face. "You did? When?"

Abby looked away and grimaced. "This morning. I—" She swallowed, having no way of explaining why it had taken so long and not thinking to ask why Erica hadn't contacted *her*.

"Abby, listen." Erica used Abby's chin to direct her gaze back to her. "I'd love to sit and talk to you. I actually have a lot to talk to you about, but there's just no time here." She rattled off the name of a hotel and the street it was on. "I'm staying there for the time being and there's a great little bar and restaurant downstairs. Maybe—" Her energy seemed to wane, along with her confidence, and she took a moment to clear her throat. "Maybe you could meet me there? And we could have dinner or drinks and—talk?"

"I'd like that," Abby answered without hesitation.

"Yeah?" Erica's relief was obvious.

"Yeah. Is tonight too soon?"

Erica's smile lit up her entire face and Abby realized sadly how rare a sight it had been in the short time they'd spent together. Sadly, because it was beautiful: her eyes shone and crinkled slightly at the corners, a subtle dimple appeared at the base of her left cheek. If Abby had been on her feet rather than sitting on the pavement, she was certain she would have swooned. "Tonight is perfect. I should be done here by six. Give me time to shower?"

"I'll be sitting at the bar by seven," Abby said.

"Great." Erica squeezed her arm. "I'll see you later."

"Later." She watched as Erica headed off in the same direction the young man had gone earlier. Only then did she notice Erica was wearing jeans. Jeans? *The queen of designer suits is working in jeans?* Her gaze drifted lower, settling on Erica's retreating backside. *Oh, my. She needs to wear jeans* all *the time.*

Yeah, something was definitely different.

"Wow. Who was that?" John was at her side, looking in the same direction as Abby, his eyes wide, his voice quiet as if he hadn't meant to actually speak aloud. When he looked at Abby and realized he had, his face flushed while Abby hid a grin.

"A friend."

"What happened?" he asked her, hurriedly changing the subject. "Are you okay?"

"Apparently, it's a good idea to actually watch where you're going when you push one of these things. Here, help me up." She held out her hand and he helped her to stand. She was already planning the timing of the evening in her head. Though she would rarely make a trip back home and then back into the city again—that'd be over two hours more in travel time alone—there was no way she was showing up for dinner with Erica dressed the way she was now, with an unidentifiable stain on her shirt and the distinctive smell of garbage emanating from her general vicinity. She mentally perused her wardrobe as she and John finished cleaning up their mess and continued on their way.

œ œ œ

Erica studied herself in the full-length mirror on the back of the door of her hotel room. Her outfit was simple, but she didn't have much choice. She hadn't brought anything dressy. She'd known she'd be working outside or in the lab or at the headquarters closer to Ground Zero and none of those places were conducive to skirts and heels. So, she'd packed accordingly. This was fine by her because she was much more comfortable in these casual clothes—she just hoped Abby wasn't disappointed.

She'd used the iron provided by the hotel to press the black slacks and now they hugged her body nicely. She'd donned a black camisole and covered that with a royal blue, full-zip sweater in a comfortable autumn weight. The combination left a nice expanse of skin at her chest, not showing cleavage but leaving lots of collarbone in view. A small diamond on a silver chain hung around her neck, matching the earrings in her lobes. She'd been wearing her hair in a ponytail since she'd arrived, to keep it out of her way, so she took this opportunity to wear it down, fluffing it a bit with her fingers, letting it skim her shoulders. A little makeup on her eyes (something she hadn't worn since she got to New York), a touch of clear lip gloss, and a spritz of her new (too expensive) perfume, and the look was complete.

Not bad, she thought, giving a curt nod to her reflection.

She tried to ignore the butterflies in her stomach as she checked the bedside clock. Seven on the dot. It was time.

Why was she so nervous? It was just Abby.

Just Abby.

She snorted. There was no such thing as "just Abby." Not in her mind. Not for the past month. She looked around the room, picked up a few scattered items, neatened her toiletries in the bathroom, made the place presentable.

"What are you doing?" she asked aloud, as she grabbed her key card and put it in her little clutch purse. "It's not like you'll be bringing her up here." As she reached for the doorknob, she swore her reflection smirked at her. "Oh, shut up," she told it.

Erica loved New York City. She loved its energy, its vitality. Before this week, she'd visited only once or twice when she was younger, but her admiration for its vivacity had stuck and seemed even stronger now. It was crushing to see the lost, pained expressions on the faces of so many people, but she had faith that they'd recover, that the entire country would recover and be stronger because of what had happened. That's why she was here, to aid in that recovery in any way she could. The people of Gander had shown her how important it was to help. It was a lesson she'd never forget and she silently thanked them for the thousandth time since her return as she rode the elevator down to the lobby.

At 7:05, Erica stood in the doorway of the restaurant/bar on the ground floor of her hotel and waited for her eyes to adjust to the dim lighting. It was busy, televisions showing sporting events and news updates, several men in suits talking and laughing. She scanned the patrons until her gaze fell on the far corner of the bar. Abby was talking with the bartender, and Erica felt the warmth of affection whoosh through her. Of *course* Abby was talking to the bartender. If not him, then the waitress or the bar-back or the guy a couple stools down. That was Abby. Erica didn't allow herself to freak out over the fact that she knew such a thing about her, that she'd recognized it, or that it filled her with fondness. Instead, she shook it all away and crossed the room.

"Hey," she said with a smile as she approached Abby.

Erica stood and Abby sat and they took each other in for several moments. Abby had changed her entire outfit and was now wearing gray slacks and a black long-sleeved shirt with big silver buttons. Small silver hoops glittered at her ears and her dark hair was glossy and loose. She looked delectable. Erica barely managed to keep herself from licking her lips. Finally, Abby stood up and opened her arms. "Hi."

Erica stepped into them and wanted to sigh at the wondrous familiarity. They hugged tightly, neither able to verbalize the sudden tenderness that enveloped them.

"You look beautiful," Abby whispered, and Erica tightened her hold.

Eyes darted away as they parted and took their seats and got comfortable. Abby signaled the bartender. "Hey, Sam," she said, as if she'd known him for years. He leaned his hands on the bar in front of them and gave Abby his full attention. He was in his late twenties with a smoothly bald head, a neatly trimmed goatee, dark skin, and kind, soft eyes.

178

"What can I get you ladies?" he asked.

"Tequila shot?" Abby asked as she turned to Erica, a twinkle in her eye.

Erica barked a laugh. "It'll be a cold day in hell before I have one of those again. Chardonnay?" she asked Sam.

"Of course." He nodded once and turned to Abby. "Another beer for you?"

"Please."

"Tequila shot," Erica chuckled, shaking her head.

"Hey, you seemed to like them in Gander." Abby shrugged.

"Hello? Am I the only one who remembers the morning after?"

"I didn't say *they* liked *you*." Sam delivered their drinks and Abby held up her beer. "It's great to see you again."

"You, too."

They touched glasses together and sipped.

"So," Erica said. "How have you been?"

"I've been all right. I've been okay."

"It has to be hard, being so close to it all."

"It has been." Abby blew out a large breath. "But it's getting better. Slowly. Very slowly. Sometimes it's two steps forward and three steps back, you know?"

Erica pressed her lips together in a thin line as Abby spoke, listening raptly. "And your mom? Is she all right?"

Abby gave a nod. "She is. It's been hard for her. She lost four friends and two spouses of friends, so that was quite a blow. She's been to way too many funerals over the past few weeks."

"I can't even begin to imagine." They were quiet for a few moments and then Erica asked, "How was San Francisco? When did you get back?"

Abby looked away and took a swig of her beer. "I didn't go."

Eyebrows raised, Erica blinked in surprise. "You didn't? How come?"

"I'm not really sure." Abby gave a half-snort.

"What happened to 'I believe in traveling the world, I am a rolling stone' and all that?" Erica's voice held no sarcasm because she was honestly curious about the answer.

179

Abby wet her lips as she searched for a way to explain something she didn't fully understand herself. "I haven't gone anywhere since we got back." Erica's expression was soft as she held Abby's gaze and Abby felt safe enough to continue. "All of my adult life, I've been about traveling and visiting and not staying in one place for too long. With the exception of that short period of time when I was working, I haven't stopped moving since I graduated from college. I never wanted to. But after 9/11, after Gander . . ." Her voice trailed off and she drained her beer, signaled to Sam for another.

"Something changed," Erica finished for her.

Abby turned and was ensnared by those crystal blue eyes. "Exactly. Something changed. I don't know what and I don't know how. I just feel different. I want to stay home. I want to be near my family. I want—" She tilted her head back and studied the square tiles of the tin ceiling. Finding the word, she looked at Erica. "Stability. I want stability."

The sip of Chardonnay in Erica's mouth went down wrong and nearly choked her. She recovered and just looked wide-eyed at Abby. "Stability?"

"I know. Right?" Abby shook her head in self-deprecation, grabbed the bottle Sam handed her and took a healthy swig.

"You? Little Miss Fly-By-The-Seat-Of-Her-Pants wants stability?"

"Don't make fun, Erica."

"I'm not." Erica touched Abby's forearm, her face sincere and her voice softening. "I promise I'm not. I'm just surprised."

Abby released a breath and gave a shrug. "I know. I can't believe it either. It's weird."

Sam set a fresh glass of wine on the bar and Erica smiled her thanks.

"You know what else is weird?" Abby asked. She caught and held Erica's eye. "I haven't told anybody that but you."

"Not even your mom?"

"Not even my mom. Though I'm sure at this point, she's starting to wonder why I'm still sticking around the house."

180

"It's not a bad thing, Abby."

"What's not?"

"Change."

"No?"

Erica shook her head as she swallowed. "No. Sometimes, it's a really good thing."

Abby studied her, full of a hundred different questions all at once. But she also wanted to slow things down, to not have her time with Erica go quite so fast. "Hey, should we order some dinner? Want to get a table?"

"I actually like this seat. Can we stay at the bar?"

With a grin, Abby said, "I like the bar, too." She caught Sam's eye and asked for menus.

Needing a break, they talked about superficial things like the weather and the quality of the hotel until their food was delivered. Once they dug in, conversation went back to more serious subjects and Abby got around to asking the question that had been on her mind since just before she'd crashed her cart earlier that day.

"So, what are you doing here?"

Erica grinned around her fork, took her time chewing. "I told you. I'm working."

"Yeah, I'm going to need a little more detail than that."

The fork clanked lightly as Erica set it on her plate, picked up her napkin from her lap, and dabbed the corners of her mouth. She sipped her wine and furrowed her brows as she thought of how to put into words what had happened to her when she returned to Raleigh from Gander.

"I was looking forward to getting back to my old life," she began, running a fingertip around the rim of her wineglass. "I really was. Gander was amazing, despite the circumstances that brought us there, but there were some things I really needed to leave behind me." She tossed a grimace in Abby's direction and Abby looked down at her lap, guilt coloring her face. "I went back to work on Monday, broke the news of my disastrous presentation to my team, and we went back to the drawing board. It was all very routine, very familiar, but I felt kind of restless." She shrugged. "I don't have a better word than that. I felt restless and I figured I was still coming down, still decompressing from everything that had happened, and that I needed to just hang in there and things would go back to normal." At that, she held Abby's gaze. "But they didn't. They wouldn't. I couldn't settle in. I didn't want to be there. For the first time in my life, I felt like I wasn't doing what I should be doing. It was so bizarre. I didn't know what to do."

"How long did this go on?" Abby asked, riveted.

"Two-and-a-half weeks—which doesn't sound like a lot, but for me? It felt like forever. Finally, I was online one night and I did a little poking around and I found chat rooms and mailing lists and online groups all made up of other people who had also been in Gander when we were there. You know, we were so isolated in our little foursome at the MacDougals that I forgot there were almost 7,000 other people marooned there as well. And it turned out a lot of them were in the same boat I was."

"What do you mean?"

"People had changed, Abby. People were changed by their experience there. Like me." Her face turned tender. "Like you."

"I don't understand."

"Of course you do. You want stability now. You said so yourself. Would you have said that a month ago on September 12th? No, you were all about traveling the world, next stop: San Francisco. And now? You don't want to go anywhere." The tone of her voice lacked any harshness, anything judgmental; she was simply stating facts. "Look at me," she went on. "A month ago, would you have thought in a million years, that I would be helping other people? That *I* would have gone to my boss and asked what our company was doing to help the residents of New York City? That I would have asked to head up the team they were sending up here to help with the anthrax research, not knowing how long we'd be staying or what we'd find once we started? Me? Really?"

"Never," Abby said, a grin beginning to form.

"That's what I mean. Some really awful, cowardly men did

something beyond despicable, but in trying to wrap our brains around such brutality, a lot of us learned new things about ourselves and a lot of us came out of it different people, better people, people more aware of what's important in life. Because if anybody learned the lesson of how short life really is, it was those of us on airplanes that day, any one of which could have been a target of the hijackers. A vicious lesson, but valuable—at least in my case."

"Change isn't always a bad thing," Abby said, repeating Erica's earlier words.

"No, it isn't."

"When did you get here?"

"Middle of last week." Erica sipped her wine, suspecting what was coming.

"You weren't going to call me." It was a simple statement and Abby's voice held no accusation, but a flash of hurt zipped across her face before she could stop it.

Erica took a deep breath. "I was waiting."

"For?"

"Some courage?"

"Some courage." Abby's dark eyebrows met above her nose, broadcasting her puzzlement.

"I didn't know what to say. I wasn't sure how to open, you know? I know we parted on good terms in the airport, but I had a tough time for a little while after that." Erica caught her bottom lip between her teeth as if embarrassed that she'd let the fact slip. "I wondered if maybe you—what had happened between us—was part of the reason I was feeling so discombobulated."

"I—" Abby started to respond, tried to come up with an apology of some sort, but Erica stopped her by laying a warm hand on her knee.

"No. No, it's okay. There's no need for you to explain. How could you? I can't explain half of what I thought or felt during those four days." She gave a soft laugh, and the genuine open smile reminded Abby once again of how seldom she'd seen it in Gander. "So, I've been biding my time, trying to figure out the

183

best approach, and suddenly there you were, crashing into a trash can right in front of my lab building."

"Ugh." Abby covered her eyes with a hand. "So embarrassing."

They shared a laugh for a moment before Erica grew more serious. "There you were," she said again. "In a city the size of New York, what are the chances we'd run into each other like that?" Erica's hand was still on Abby's knee and she squeezed gently. "I'm a scientist, Abby. I don't believe in God. I've never believed in Fate or Destiny or any of those things, but I don't know how else to explain it. The chances of us meeting in a city this size are just too slim and yet—"

"Here we are," Abby said.

"Here we are."

"My mom always says everything happens for a reason," Abby commented as she popped a steak fry into her mouth.

"Mine, too."

"I always thought that was just some superstitious way of explaining things she had no explanation for, but now I have to wonder. First we meet in Gander. Now here. It *is* kind of weird."

"It's totally weird. But in a good way." Erica finished her salad and pushed her dish away, as did Abby.

Sam was on the scene immediately, clearing dishes away and wiping down the bar. "Can I get you ladies anything else?"

"How do you feel about coffee?" Abby asked, not wanting the evening to end.

"Coffee sounds great."

They sat in comfortable, companionable silence for long moments, sipping their coffee and tossing tender smiles at each other, simply content to be sitting next to each other. On occasion, Erica would wave at a fellow patron. She explained to Abby that there were ten employees from her company staying there.

"Our lab is very close. It wasn't easy to find a hotel near Ground Zero that was repaired and ready to put us up, but this one's been pretty great."

They talked about the other buildings damaged when the towers collapsed and how it would be months before most of them were up and running again, but how incredible the amount of effort from people had been. Neither of them had ever experienced such teamwork, and it was inspiring.

They continued to sit at the bar, long after they'd put a stop to the coffee refills, watching as patrons left one by one, until only a handful were left. Finally, Abby reluctantly glanced at her watch and sighed.

"Wow. It's getting late. I should probably get going." Her voice betrayed her; the last thing she sounded like was that she wanted to get going.

Erica kept her eyes on her empty coffee cup and nibbled on her lip for several seconds before working up the nerve to speak. "Abby?"

"Hmm?"

"Would you—" She cleared her throat, then forced herself to look up, to look Abby directly in those big, beautiful blue eyes. "Would you be interested in coming up to my room with me?"

Chapter 19

Neither spoke during the elevator ride up, but Erica and Abby stood very close together against the back wall. When the doors slid open, Erica led and Abby followed, still no words, nothing but absolute certainty.

Abby hadn't felt as solid in four weeks as she did right now and she had no idea how to explain it. It had never occurred to her that she might have feelings for Erica, feelings other than carnal ones—thinking about that now, she felt a little stupid, a little childish. How could it not cross her mind? All the signs were there. In general, when she slept with somebody with no intention of anything more, that person was fairly easily forgotten soon after the encounter. Certainly within a month. But not Erica. Abby couldn't get Erica out of her head no matter how hard she tried. How could she not even consider that maybe there was something deeper going on?

Probably because something deeper than sex was pretty much a foreign concept to her.

For her part, Erica was a bit further along in her self-analysis, but not a lot less surprised by the turn of events. She knew she had feelings for Abby; she'd known it when they'd parted in the airport four weeks ago. There was no certainty about how they'd developed, especially given that Abby was nothing like the women she was usually drawn to, but there was a certainty that Abby did not feel the same way and so Erica had dealt with this matter of the heart privately and alone, assuming they'd pass eventually as long as she kept busy doing something satisfying. So she had, and it seemed like it had been working—until today. She'd seen Abby and it was as if four weeks had disappeared. Now, all she wanted was to feel the way she'd felt in the MacDougals' basement a month earlier. She had no intention of spilling her guts about emotions and feelings. She simply wanted to be in Abby's arms again, to let the world fall away for one night, to spend a few hours in a place where she felt safe and warm and like she could be herself.

Erica's hotel room was warm. She dropped her key card on the dresser, kicked off her shoes, and drew the sheers across the window, obscuring the room to watchful eyes, but allowing the lights of New York City to be seen. Not for the first time, she was grateful the hotel faced a direction that would not emphasize the gaping hole in the skyline left by the towers.

Abby came up behind her, the warm length of her body pressing along Erica's back, her lean arms wrapping around Erica's torso. She remembered then how well they fit together, snugly, like two pieces of a puzzle. Erica crossed her arms over Abby's at her stomach and they stood looking out the window, completely content in each other's presence.

After long moments, Abby spoke. "You're different," she said quietly.

"I know. Is that a good thing or a bad thing?"

"I think that's a trick question," Abby said and she felt Erica's quiet laughter against her. "It just feels like you're more you."

Erica turned in Abby's arms and looked up into her face, confused. "What do you mean?"

Choosing her words carefully was important right now, Abby knew. The last time she'd tried to describe Erica's change in demeanor, it had stung her, even though that hadn't been Abby's intention. "I feel like this is the real you and you're not trying to play some part; you're not worried about image or perception. You seem comfortable in your own skin and I don't think you were in Gander." She rolled her lips in and bit down on them, waiting for Erica's reaction.

To Abby's surprise, Erica said simply, "You're right. You're different, too, you know."

"I know, and I never even realized it until today. What an idiot I am."

187

"Nah," Erica said. "You just didn't have somebody to point it out until today."

"Hmm. I like your explanation better." Abby kissed Erica, softly, with tenderness, taking her time, absorbing the feelings of warmth, comfort, and the underlying promise of passion. When she pulled back, the two of them held each other's gaze.

After a moment, Erica said quietly, "I'm glad you're here," and stroked a finger down the side of Abby's face.

"So am I."

Their lips met again, but they were in no hurry. Abby unzipped Erica's sweater, pushed it off her shoulders, and stood in reverence at the sight before her. Erica's black bra and camisole, black slacks, and bare feet stole the air from Abby's lungs and she held her at arm's length.

"Just let me look at you for a minute," she whispered as she took in the sight. Erica was gorgeous.

A few short moments passed before Erica said, "My turn," and set to work on the silver buttons of Abby's blouse.

Down to bras and underwear, they stumbled to the bed and fell across it, lips fused together, hands grasping, sliding, exploring. They took their time, wanting to learn and see and touch everything and every part of each other. Abby gently slipped one strap off Erica's shoulder, then the other, tugging the fabric down to reveal breasts even more beautiful than she remembered. Erica's skin was still as soft and still as smooth as it had been a month earlier, and Abby sighed with great contentment as she tasted a shoulder, licked a collarbone, sucked in a nipple. Positioning herself above Erica, with one thigh between Erica's legs, Abby settled in. She lavished attention on one breast, then on the other, moving back and forth between them slowly and easily, like she had all the time in the world. Every so often, she'd push against Erica's center with her thigh, basking in the subtle intake of breath that came as a result, loving the wet heat she could feel even through the fabric of Erica's panties.

Erica thought she might explode from the wanting. She couldn't recall a time when her body had been so alive, so aflame, simply from Abby's hot mouth on her breasts, bathing her skin and erotically torturing each nipple, gently with her lips and tongue, a bit more roughly with her teeth. None of her past lovers had ever taken such time with, such pleasure in, her body. It was pushing Erica's arousal to unfamiliar heights and seemed to go on and on, simultaneously sensual and agonizingly teasing, until she finally reached her breaking point and did something she'd never done in bed before.

With anybody.

Ever.

She begged.

"Please? Abby? Please?" Her voice was a hoarse whisper.

Abby didn't look up, continued what she was doing, switching mouth for fingers as she remarked, "You have the most amazing breasts I have ever seen."

"Abby," Erica whimpered. "You're killing me here. Please?"

"Seriously. They're the perfect size, not too big, not too small. And your skin is so soft. And your nipples—" She squeezed one between her thumb and forefinger, wrenching a groan from Erica's throat. "They're just—"

Erica grabbed a handful of Abby's hair and forced her head up as she lifted her own, so they were eye to eye before she growled, "Abby," through clenched teeth.

A devilish grin crossed Abby's face as she quickly slid her hand down the front of Erica's panties, through the coarse hair and into the slick heat waiting for her there.

Erica dropped her head back onto the bed as a primal groan bubbled up from her chest. "Oh, yes," she breathed, easing her grip on Abby's hair, but not letting go. "Oh, Abby. Thank you."

"Um, no. Thank *you*."

As with the first time they'd been together, Abby suddenly found herself wanting to slow down, wanting to transform seconds into minutes, minutes into hours, wanting never to leave the warmth of the bed she was in or the feel of the woman beneath her. Only this time, she understood what it meant. She understood that this was more than just sex, that Erica was more than just another woman she'd bedded, and this time when they kissed, Abby tried to telegraph those thoughts to Erica, tried to tell her that this was an important moment, that she was beginning to understand. She slowed the pace of her fingers, knowing Erica wasn't going to last much longer but hoping to milk the moment for all she could. She kissed Erica passionately, but with a tenderness she usually avoided. Shifting her body forced Erica to spread her legs more fully and Abby tucked her hips between them, the added pressure from her pelvis against her hand pulling more erotic sounds from Erica's throat. Abby rocked gently but insistently, feeling blissful pleasure as Erica's heel dug into the back of her thigh, as Erica's hips pushed up to meet Abby's hand. She knew Erica was dangerously close to the edge and was on a direct path to take her over when she was abruptly hit with the inexplicable desire for eye contact. A flash of memory zapped her then, Erica's voice from four weeks ago echoing in Abby's head.

"Keep your eyes open. Look at me."

And in that moment, like a light switch had been turned on in a previously dark room, she got it. It was clear. Abby now understood what Erica had been saying then. Unlike the last time they were together, this meeting of bodies was more than the simple act of sex. The last time, it was about feeling life, feeling desire, *feeling* anything. This time, it was about them, about being together, about understanding—or at least beginning to understand—that there was something deeper between them. Something stronger. Something unnerving. And at that moment, the most important thing in the world to Abby was that Erica know who was with her, who was driving her pleasure—not who was fucking her but who was *making love* to her.

"Erica."

Erica's head was thrown back on the pillow, eyes closed, one hand pushing against the headboard, completely absorbed in what her body was feeling.

Abby slowed her rhythm to a near stop. "Erica."

190

Erica whimpered a protest, blinked rapidly, and focused on Abby, who looked at her tenderly and whispered, "Look at me. Keep your eyes open and look at me. Okay?"

Erica's eyes welled as the words registered in her arousal-addled brain, and she laid her palm against Abby's cheek, rubbed her thumb over Abby's bottom lip, and gave an almost imperceptible nod.

They kissed then. Sweetly. Lovingly. And Abby began moving again while Erica looked in her eyes. A slow, easy rocking, a slow, easy stroking, Abby's gaze riveted on Erica's as they held tightly to each other, both painfully aware that something important had passed between them.

They moved in tandem, crested together, and fell over the edge as one.

ଓ ଓ ଓ

Hours later, Abby lay in an exhausted heap on the twisted sheets, sweating, breathless, and feeling like a Gumby doll with limbs of rubber. She lifted her arm from over her eyes and watched Erica walk across the room from the bathroom, carrying a glass of water, in all her naked glory. Abby stopped her with an upheld hand, like a traffic cop.

"Wait."

Erica halted and looked around. "What? What's the matter?"

"Just stand there for a second."

Erica rolled her eyes and continued on her path. "Here. Drink this before you dehydrate."

"You're gorgeous."

"So are you."

Abby gulped down half the glass as Erica crawled into bed beside her, offered the remaining water to Erica who polished it off. They rearranged the covers, rearranged their bodies, and settled into a comfortable cocoon made up of each other. It would be a while—an hour or two—before the sun began to crest over the horizon, and they lay together, wrapped in each other, facing the window, Erica's head tucked under Abby's chin. Erica yawned and Abby kissed her forehead.

"Tired?"

"Exhausted. You wiped me out."

"That's the pot calling the kettle black. I can barely feel my legs."

Erica reached down to Abby's calf and stroked her fingertips up the inside of her leg, feather-lightly, until she hit the apex between Abby's thighs and made her jump. "Legs are still there," she informed her.

"Good to know." Abby tightened her arm around Erica's shoulders.

They lay in the quiet, warm and sated, for long moments. Erica had just begun to doze when Abby spoke, her voice barely above a whisper.

"Erica?"

"Hmm?"

"What happens now?"

There were many ways to interpret that question, many inferences Erica could make about what *exactly* Abby was asking her. Instead of assuming—which is what she'd done a month ago and what had gotten her painfully slapped down—she decided to play dumb.

"What do you mean?"

"I mean—" Abby shifted slightly beneath her and cleared her throat. "I mean, what do we do next?"

"Hmm."

Abby waited.

"Well, I have to work in less than four hours, so we could sleep next. That might be good."

"Very funny. That's not what I meant and you know it."

"Oh. Hmm," Erica said again.

Abby turned to squint at her, trying to read Erica's face in the dark. "Are you making fun of me?"

Erica chuckled.

"You are! You're totally making fun of me. I can't believe you're mocking me when I'm trying to be serious here."

Erica pushed herself up on her forearms so she could look down and study Abby's face. "You're right," she said and then placed a gentle kiss on Abby's cheek. "I'm sorry." She propped her chin in one hand and asked, "What are you being serious about?"

"About us," Abby said, pouring obvious frustration into those two words. "I'm being serious about us."

"Us, huh?" Erica's gaze moved to the window as she considered what to say next, in which direction to take the conversation. All the options terrified her.

Abby altered her position, sitting up in the bed to lean against the headboard. She reached toward the nightstand, clicked on the lamp there, and they both blinked in the sudden illumination. "I mean, there is an us, right? I feel like—isn't there an us?"

Abby's voice wavered just a touch and Erica felt her insides warm at the sound. She looked up into Abby's face, into her eyes, and saw nothing but trust and sincerity—both the things she'd hoped to see four weeks earlier. She hadn't expected them to scare her then, but they did now, so she tossed the ball back into Abby's court.

"I don't know," she said. "Is there?"

Abby sifted Erica's hair through her fingers, touched her face. "Yeah. I think there is."

Erica rolled onto her back so her head was in Abby's lap. She took Abby's hand in both her own and toyed with it as she spoke, entwining and then untwining their fingers. "Why?"

Abby blinked at her. "Why?"

"Yeah. Why now? Why is there an us now but there wasn't an us in Gander?" Erica's voice held no accusation, no anger, merely curiosity, and Abby nodded. She understood what was going on; Erica was a scientist, after all. A scientist who liked—no, she *needed*—concrete answers.

"You said it yourself many times downstairs," Abby began, speaking slowly, trying the words on for size as she spoke them, thinking out loud. "That situation, that place, those people changed us. Probably all of us. I just didn't know it at the time, but I think you did."

"Changed you how?"

Smiling down into Erica's face, brushing her hair off her forehead, Abby admired her tenacity. *She's going to make me say it. She wants me to say it all. Good for her.* "I believe in traveling. I believe in seeing as much of the world as I can. That hasn't changed. But—" She tilted her head back as if the words for which she searched might be found on the ceiling. "My priorities have. The things that are important to me have shifted."

"What used to be first?"

"Being happy and having fun. Not allowing myself to be tied down."

"And what's first now?"

"My family and friends." She looked down into Erica's eyes. "The people I care about."

Erica nodded slowly, seemingly satisfied.

"What about you?" Abby asked, turning the tables, which was only fair. "Have your priorities shifted, too?"

"Absolutely."

"What used to be first?"

Erica gave a snort. "Me. Always me."

"And now?"

"Not me." She laughed, then continued. "Others. People. Animals. The less fortunate. The ones I can help. My family." She mirrored Abby, looked her in the eye. "The people who matter to me."

Abby leaned down and placed a gentle kiss on Erica's mouth. When she sat back up, she said softly, "Correct me if I'm wrong, but—" She swallowed audibly. "I think we could have something here. You and me. Something good."

If Erica had learned anything about Abby in the short time they'd known each other, it was that saying something with such implications about the future was extremely hard for her, was extremely *rare* for her. Bringing Abby's hand to her lips, she kissed the tip of each finger before looking back up at her and asking, "So? What do we do about it?"

June 14, 2002
Friday

Chapter 20

"Are you sure I look all right?" Corinne MacDougal asked.

"Mom, you look great," Kate MacDougal replied from the driver's seat of her mother's car, shaking her head. "Just like you did the last fourteen times you asked me."

Despite her daughter's reassurances, Corinne pulled the visor down and peered critically into the tiny mirror.

Kate smothered an amused grin. Her mother was never this self-conscious. Never. Sure, she liked to look nice, but she never got crazy. As she liked to say, "I've been married to your father for thirty years. Who've I got to impress?" But Kate watched out of the corner of her eye as her mother fussed with her hair, smoothed her eyebrows, and then applied more lipstick.

"Mom," she said, a bit more forcefully. When Corinne looked at her, Kate smiled widely. "You look great. I promise."

Corinne patted her daughter's arm. "Thanks, honey. I don't know why I'm so nervous."

Kate knew. She'd been on the other side of the country, but she'd heard all about that incredible week.

It had been nine months and now Kate's mother was about to have dinner with the four Plane People she called her own. Corinne wasn't the only one with a case of the nerves; Kate just hid it better. She'd heard endless stories about Brian-this and Erica-that and Michael-said-this and Abby-helped-with-that. Her parents' voices were uncharacteristically animated for weeks after all the unexpected guests had left, and they still were on occasion. Kate was anxious to meet this foursome. She felt like she already knew them. She knew she'd thrown a wrench in her mother's gears when she decided to come home to meet them; if she hadn't, Corinne probably would have wanted to put them all up in the house again. Warmth flooded her as she realized, not for the first time, what a terrific grandmother her mom was going to make one day.

The afternoon was beautiful, sunny, and mild, with a gentle breeze blowing off the water. Kate loved Vancouver, loved the hustle and bustle of it, and was very happy there, but there was something calming about being back home in the little town of Gander. Yes, she had moved to the big city, but not because she didn't love the quiet country. Truth was, she missed it much more than she'd expected to when she left in the first place. A deep breath of fresh Gander air filled her heart just as surely as it filled her lungs.

The parking lot of the Hotel Gander was almost full to capacity, something that rarely happened. But it was a special weekend; the Plane People had many different chat groups and websites online and some of them had planned a big get-together—the first of what they hoped would turn out to be an annual event. Many people had come for visits on their own before now, but this was a large undertaking. Passengers from four different flights had made arrangements to meet, have an outdoor gathering, contact their hosts or the locals they'd met during their unexpected stop here. The Hotel Gander seemed to have the majority of the attendees. Plus, there was Tomcats Bar and Grill downstairs where everybody could mingle. With no idea of how many people planned to show up, Kate circled until she found a spot, then slid the car into Park.

"Dad said he'd meet us inside as soon as he could," she said, turning to her mother. Corinne's uncharacteristic quiet was a clue to how edgy she was. "You ready?"

Inside was buzzing. People of every size, shape, color, and nationality mingled, drank, hugged, and laughed. Glasses clinked. Slaps on the back reverberated through the spacious room. Every so often, a squeal of delight pierced the air and somebody fell into somebody else's arms. It was like a family reunion—where the family consisted of a couple hundred people.

Corinne's face went from uncertain to sunny as she looked around, recognizing faces she'd held near and dear for the past ten months. Before she could take in more, two large hands slipped around from behind her and covered her eyes.

"You look even more beautiful than I remember," a low, male voice said in her ear.

Corinne laughed and slapped at the body in back of her. When he let go, she turned around and her eyes filled with tears. "Brian."

"Hello, Gorgeous."

They hugged tightly and Kate felt a rush of warmth at the gentleness with which Brian held her mother. When they parted, he turned his soft green eyes in her direction and held out his hand.

"You must be Kate," he said, his smile showing even, white teeth.

"I am," she said as she took his outstretched hand and he clasped hers with both of his.

His sandy hair was neat. He was clean-shaven and he looked her in the eye as he said, "I see your mother passed on her beauty to her daughter." *Corny, but in a charming way,* she thought, and made a mental note to berate her mother for not warning her about this one. His rugged cuteness, his enticing voice—her stomach flip-flopped.

"I can't believe how many people are here," Corinne said, looking around in amazement.

"It's pretty incredible," Brian said with a nod. "Just goes to show how much this place means to us. Where's Tim?"

"He'll be here soon. Have you seen the others yet?"

She didn't have to elaborate for Brian to know who she meant. "Abby should be down any minute. Erica's flight was late." He looked around, craned his neck. "Michael's got our table over that way—there he is." He waved an arm above his head and in less than thirty seconds, Corinne was enveloped in yet another heartfelt hug.

"My lord, it's good to see you," Michael said as he held

199

Corinne at arms' length. Stepping aside, he ushered a small slip of a woman into the circle. "Corinne MacDougal, this is my wife, Gwen."

Gwen took Corinne's hand in hers. "How do you do? I've heard so much about you," she said, a sparkle in her brown eyes. "It's nice to finally meet you."

They fell into an easy group conversation, asking for updates, talking about family. The internet had allowed them to keep up at least a little bit with one another's lives. Sometimes, time got away from them and too many weeks went by between contacts, but they'd done their best to make the effort.

As they moved across the room toward their table, Corinne reflected on what she knew about the current lives of each of them. Brian had settled into bachelorhood fairly well. He didn't like it; he was a man who preferred to be married, but he sounded much better over the past few months—about dating, about love, about life in general—than he had when he'd been in Gander last year. She watched out of the corner of her eye and smothered a satisfied grin, knowing very well the expression that graced her daughter's face as she and Brian chatted. *Oh, yes, this is going to be interesting.* She knew Michael and Gwen had celebrated their twenty-fifth wedding anniversary with a vacation in Paris, something they'd been talking about for years but had never gotten around to. She knew Erica had moved to a different department within her company, heading up their division dealing with charity and donations and was now much happier in this new capacity (a revelation that both stunned Corinne and made her inexplicably proud of the girl). She'd also decided to get herself a cat, which she adopted from a local shelter, and she always asked Corinne about Sammy. Corinne tried to send pictures as often as she could. Lastly, she knew Abby'd had a job interview recently, but she hadn't given a lot of details because, as she'd told Corinne, she didn't want to jinx it. She also knew Abby was dating some-body new, but got no details there either and for the same reason. While Corinne was happy for Abby simply because she sounded happy (if one could actually sound *happy* via e-mail), she was the slightest bit disappointed. Tim often said she was a hopeless romantic, but Corinne was sure she had seen something spark between Abby and Erica and she had hoped the two of them would find each other. But Abby was flighty and Erica was stoic and maybe if they'd had more than four days together, things would have been different.

Oh, well, she thought as she returned her focus to the people around her. She was over the moon about being able to see them again, regardless. "So," she said to Gwen and Michael as they all took seats, "tell me all about Paris."

ભ ભ ભ

Abby's watch read five minutes later than the last time she'd checked it. Her hair looked exactly the same as it had when she'd looked in the mirror last, a minute before she'd checked her watch last.

"Where is she?" she asked aloud as she flopped back down onto the bed. Erica's flight had been delayed, but had landed and she was on her way, should be there any time.

It never ceased to amaze Abby how nervously excited she got every time she was going to see Erica. They'd been doing the long distance thing since the previous October, and while it wasn't always easy, it seemed to be working for them. After much discussion, they had agreed to try their best to avoid the standard lesbian process of U-Hauling immediately after they'd realized they had feelings. This was a relief, especially to Abby, who hadn't been in any type of significant, exclusive relationship in—ever, really. Long-distance dating would be a good test.

Imagine her surprise when their once-a-month visits started to feel like less than enough for Abby.

It had been almost three weeks since their last visit and Abby was feeling like a junkie who needed a fix. Badly.

They were going to have to talk about this.

Because Abby had a solution.

With a sigh, she reached for the TV remote just as there was

201

a light tap on the door. She flew to it so fast, she wasn't sure her feet actually touched the carpet.

Before Erica could utter a hello—or even register that it was, in fact, Abby who'd answered the door—she was yanked inside, slammed bodily against the door, and subjected to a determined plundering of her mouth. Her bag slid off her shoulder and fell to the floor with a thump as she let go of everything she was holding onto so she could cup Abby's face in her hands and give back as good as she was getting.

When they finally parted, flushed and breathless, they stood with their foreheads pressed together.

"Hi," Abby whispered.

"Hi," Erica replied just as quietly.

"You're late."

"I know. I'm sorry."

"I'm torn right now." Abby brushed Erica's hair back from her face.

"Between?"

"Getting us downstairs where everybody already is because they're probably wondering where the hell we are, and ripping every stitch of clothing from your body with my teeth."

Erica's swallow was audible and Abby kissed her again. After several minutes, she wrenched their lips apart, holding Abby's mouth away with some effort. "Okay, how about this: we go downstairs, visit, eat because I'm starving, and when we get back up here tonight, you can have your way with me. Deal?"

Abby feigned a pout, but relented and let Erica take quick stock of herself in the bathroom while she waited on the bed.

"Have you seen anybody yet?" Erica called from the sink.

"I had a cocktail with Mr. Baker a little while ago." Abby saw him and his wife on a fairly regular basis at home, so visiting with him here was just an added bonus. It was hard to see him alone, though.

"He made it? I wasn't sure if he would. It can't be easy for him to be here. I completely understand why Mrs. Baker decided not to attend."

"Yeah, they seem to be hanging in there, but it's rough. He wanted to be here, said he felt like he owed it to the MacDougals, and she agreed, but couldn't bring herself to tag along. Too painful. Maybe next time."

Erica exited the bathroom and stood before Abby. "Ready?"

Abby hadn't really even looked at her before she'd pounced, so she took the opportunity now. Soft denim jeans, a white Henley, and brown sandals made for an understated yet classy outfit. Erica had taken to wearing little to no makeup and Abby thought she was even more beautiful because of it. Her hair was a little shorter than it had been last October, but still the rich coppery-red, and there was something in her eyes that Abby had grown used to, but which she knew the others would see as different, something solid and confident.

"You're stunning," she said and meant it, as she stood and took Erica's hand in hers.

Erica looked down at their entwined fingers, then up at Abby, an eyebrow arched in question.

"Is this okay?" Abby squeezed.

"I was going to ask you the same thing."

They'd kept their relationship under wraps, at least from their fellow Plane People as well as the MacDougals, because, to be honest, neither of them was sure it would work. But it had been nine months and Erica had become much too important to Abby to pretend. Abby's expression was one of radiance, her face lit up as she gave Erica a quick kiss on the mouth. "Let's go."

 os os os

Many people in the crowd at Tomcats stopped in mid-conversation to watch when Abby squealed and launched herself at Brian, wrapping her arms and legs around him like some kind of monkey, laughing and hugging and pecking kisses all over his face. He was just as delighted to see her and spun them in a circle. Erica shook her head with a grin, taking in those at the table, feeling so warm and content inside that her eyes misted.

203

Michael was up first, wrapping Erica up in a heartfelt hug. "Hello, love," he said softly in her ear. "You look fantastic."

So did he. His face glowed as he introduced her to Gwen. Next to her was Kate MacDougal, looking very much like a pretty, feminine version of her father with strawberry blond hair and a sprinkling of freckles across the bridge of her nose. Her eyes held the same inherent kindness as her mother's.

"I've heard so much about you," she said to Erica.

"And I, you. Thanks so much for the use of your room, by the way." A tap on her shoulder made her turn and there was Brian. He swooped her up as Abby greeted Michael.

"Hey, Red," Brian said.

"Brian. You look great."

"I feel great," he said, and his green eyes twinkled.

Abby was now hugging Corinne and Erica waited her turn, her heart swelling as she saw a tear spill down Corinne's cheek. She let go of Abby and immediately grabbed Erica.

"It's so good to see you," she said, her voice cracking.

Erica held her tightly. "You, too. I've missed you."

They spent the next few hours laughing and drinking and catching up. Erica looked around the room, scanning the faces, amazed by how many people were there and even more amazed by the fact that this was a mere fraction of the total number of people who went through the same experience those at her table had. From the online chat rooms, she knew that everybody wanted to do things, to take steps to say thank you to the residents of Gander who'd been so kind and generous during their stay. Passengers from the flights that had been housed in the local schools had created scholarship funds to help students there. Erica's flight had taken up a collection to get the Lions Club new appliances for its kitchen. All the passengers who'd had pets looked after by locals were giving a large donation to the local animal shelter. And tomorrow, there was a picnic at a nearby park where a monument was being erected as a gift to the residents of Gander from the Plane People.

The atmosphere was thick with joy and happiness and once again, she was struck by the fact that an event so awful had led her to meet some of the most incredible people on the planet, people she knew would be part of her life forever.

As conversation continued and alcohol flowed, Abby and Erica touched like any couple would, finally unconcerned about making their relationship known. Abby laid a hand on Erica's knee as she leaned over to talk with Corinne. Erica toyed with the ends of Abby's hair as they listened to Michael tell the story of how he and Gwen had met.

Brian and Corinne exchanged a knowing look at one point, then grinned like fools.

Abby tipped toward Erica a little later and asked, "How long before Brian asks Kate out?"

"There will be a date planned by the end of the night," Erica said. "I'm certain of it."

"I don't know, they say that long-distance thing never works out."

Erica turned to her. "Well, *they* are obviously mistaken."

Abby held her gaze for a moment, then said, "I'm happy here."

"Me, too."

"I love Gander. I really do. There's something about it—" She tapped her chest with one finger. "I feel it here. You know?"

Erica squeezed her knee. "I do."

They watched the room, scanned their own table, reveled in being around people who made them feel warm, loved, like family.

A realization hit Erica then and she turned to Abby. "Hey, hear anything about the job?" Abby hadn't given her many details about the interview she'd had the previous week, said she didn't want to jinx it.

"I got it." Abby bit her bottom lip.

Erica blinked. "What?"

"I got the job."

"Oh, my god, that's great!" Erica said, practically squealing. The others stopped their conversations and looked. "Abby got the job she interviewed for last week," Erica told them.

"That's terrific, Abby," Claire said, her face lit up. "Can you tell us about it now?"

"She didn't give you any specifics either?" Erica asked with a good-natured roll of her eyes.

"She was afraid of jinxing it," Brian told her.

"So I heard."

They all turned expectantly to Abby.

She wet her lips, nodding slowly. *Moment of truth,* she thought, though she hadn't expected it to take place in front of everybody. "It's a small, up-and-coming company that a friend of a friend turned me on to. There's some great potential and it'll be an opportunity for me to use my degree again. Finally. Which will make my parents very happy."

Chuckles went around the table.

"Good for you," Michael said.

"Whereabouts is it?" Erica asked, sipping her wine.

Abby cleared her throat. "The company's in Raleigh." She immediately took a swig of her beer, afraid to look at Erica, though she could feel her eyes on her. The rest of the table had gone quiet, as if everybody was bracing for a reaction. If it had been unclear to anybody what was going on between the two women, it was apparent now.

"You mean," Erica began, having a hard time stating the obvious. "You mean, you'll be working in Raleigh?"

Abby nodded, still not able to look her in the face. Instead, she spoke to her beer bottle. "I'll get a little apartment, don't worry. I don't want to crowd you We can each have our own lives. If you want. I'm good with that as long as it means—" She swallowed hard and finally shifted her gaze to meet Erica's. Her words came out in a long stream of run-on sentences, as if she was afraid to give Erica any room to speak, lest she bring it all crashing down. "As long as it means I can be closer to you. I know we promised to take things slowly and we have and it's been good. But, Erica, once a month is hard. Isn't it hard for you? It's hard for me. It's really hard for me. It's harder than I thought it would be. When I'm with you, not only am I ridiculously happy, but I'm content. I feel safe and sure, like it's the way things are supposed to be. And when I'm not with you, I'm waiting until the next time I will be. So once a month, I'm giddy and ecstatic and the other three weeks I spend in limbo. And I don't want to do that any more. I want to be with you. It doesn't have to be all the time, because I know that might freak you out, but I want to see you more often. I *need* to see you more often. Once a month isn't enough for me. I need to see you more and oh my god could I just shut up now?" She covered her face with her hand and shook her head slowly back and forth, bracing for the wrath of Erica.

Instead, she felt warm fingers prying her own hand off her face, then using her chin to turn her head so she faced Erica. Erica, whose crystal blue eyes were misty and shining. In that moment, everybody else at the table, the room, the entire hotel simply fell away. There was nothing, there was nobody but Erica, holding her by the chin and smiling at her.

"Abby?" she said, her voice barely above a whisper.

"Hm?"

"Answer me one question. Okay?"

Abby nodded once. "Okay."

"Why?"

Brows furrowed. "Why? Why what?"

"Why do you need to see me more often?"

A slow grin began to creep across Abby's face as she thought, not for the first time, *She's going to make me say it.* Surprisingly, it didn't scare her. It didn't freak her out. It didn't make her feel like she was breaking out in hives. Rather, it felt like the next logical step. It felt like the truth. It felt right. She cleared her throat as if about to make an important announcement.

"I need to see you more often because I am in love with you, Erica." A delighted gasp issued from Corinne and Abby had to stifle a smile. "I am in love with you and once a month is not often enough to see the person you're in love with. That's why."

"Sounds like a damn good reason to me," Brian said, raising his glass over the table. "To being in love."

As the table clinked glass against glass and made statements of "hear, hear," and "cheers," Erica stroked a fingertip down the side of Abby's face, stunned, impressed, and relieved by her admission. She'd been wondering. She'd been waiting. She'd been patient, letting Abby set the pace for the relationship, but she'd been getting restless, wondering what the next step should be. Wondering if there even was a next step for them, hoping there was, but afraid to ask, afraid to push. And today, Abby had grabbed her by the hand and taken her there.

"Well?" Abby said quietly as the friends around them fell back into conversation.

"Well what?" Erica teased.

Abby rolled her eyes. "You're killing me here. You know that, right?"

Erica laughed, squeezed Abby's thigh. "I know. I'm sorry."

"So, what do you think? About what I said."

"Honestly, there really is only one response I can give."

Abby chewed on the inside of her cheek, bracing.

Erica's face broke into a wide smile. "I love you, too."

Georgia Beers was born and raised in upstate New York, on the coast of Lake Ontario and just a short drive from the wine country of the Finger Lakes. The winner of one Lambda Literary Award and two Golden Crown Literary Awards, she is the eldest of five daughters and has been writing since she was old enough to hold a pen. When not writing, she watches too much TV, goes to matinees alone (introverts like to do that), reads voraciously, and invents new reasons not to go to the gym.

Georgia lives in Rochester, New York, with her partner of seventeen years, her teenage niece, two dogs, and a cat. Find out more at www.georgiabeers.com.

Bywater Books

The Indelible Heart

MARIANNE K. MARTIN

"Marianne Martin is a skilled writer who fully develops her characters and pulls the best from them."

—Mega Scene Book Review

Ten years ago, Charlie Crawford shot dead his two lesbian neighbors. Sharon Davis was their avenging angel, the woman who fought to win justice for her murdered friends.

But justice didn't ease the pain. Beer did, though. And Sharon's love for the bottle cost her the love of her partner Laura. Laura's departure was the cue for the descent into depression that finally forced Sharon to rebuild her shattered life.

Now the past is back with a vengeance. Charlie Crawford is terminally ill and seeking early release on compassionate grounds. Sharon has to fight for justice all over again.

When Laura comes back to town, Sharon's history threatens to overwhelm her. Hate nearly destroyed her ten years before. Has Sharon learned enough about love and friendship since then to keep herself whole this time?

The Indelible Heart reintroduces Sage and Deanne, and Kasey and Connie, from the best selling *Love in the Balance*.

Paperback Original | ISBN 978-1-932859-77-5 | $14.95

Bywater Books

Shaken and Stirred

JOAN OPYR

"What a great read! Character, story, dialogue—it's a trifecta of a page turner." —Kate Clinton, author of *I Told You So*

"Opyr is a master of mixing light and dark—of telling a story about family dysfunction, alcoholic rage and life without a lover with laugh-out loud panache." —*Book Marks*

"*Shaken and Stirred* is a fine, entertaining read, dealing with family complexity, the longings and ruminations that revisiting your childhood home can bring and a very unexpected love story. It's a wonderful novel" —*Out in Print*

Poppy Koslowski is trying to recover from a hysterectomy, but her family has other ideas. She's the one with the responsibility to pull the plug on her alcoholic grandfather in North Carolina. So she's dragged back across the country from her rebuilt life into the bosom of a family who barely notice the old man's imminent death.

Plunged into a crazy kaleidoscope of consulting doctors, catching fire with an old flame, and negotiating lunch venues with her mother and grandmother, Poppy still manages to fall in love. Because nothing in the Koslowski family is ever straight forward. Not even dying.

Paperback Original | ISBN 978-1-932859-79-9 | $14.95

Available at your local bookstore
or call 734-662-8815
or order online at www.bywaterbooks.com

Bywater Books

The Girls Club

SALLY BELLEROSE

"In her debut novel, Bellerose deftly tells the story of Cora Rose, Marie, and Renee LaBarre, a trio of working-class sisters in small-town Massachusetts who are best friends, mortal enemies, and forever loyal to each other. . . . A fast-paced, well-written tale with characters who will linger in the reader's memory long after the final page is turned."
—*Publishers Weekly*

"Bellerose moves these wonderous creations of hers through the ordinary pitfalls of life, showcasing their heartbreaks, their triumphs and their shame with equal assurance. *The Girls Club* is an incredible book—not just for girls, but for everyone." —*Out in Print*

"Winner of the Bywater Prize for Fiction, this first novel provides an intense study of human frailty and hope; sure to appeal to readers who enjoy literate coming-of-age and coming-out fiction." —*Library Journal*

"Bellerose's warm novel embraces the concept of sisterhood with propulsive gusto" —*Book Marks*

Paperback Original | ISBN 978-1-932859-78-2 | $14.95

Available at your local bookstore
or call 734-662-8815
or order online at www.bywaterbooks.com

Bywater Books

Camptown Ladies

MARI SANGIOVANNI

"Damn if I didn't actually laugh out loud while reading it —several times, in fact. If you're looking for a funny, well-written novel . . . give this a try!" —AfterEllen.com

Just when you thought it was safe to pitch your tent, the Santora family shows up. Lisa's taken over a rundown campground, baby sister Marie's been dumped (again!) by the actress, and the Santoras don't know the meaning of minding their own business. When the whole clan decides to fix things for their girls, it's a hilarious recipe for havoc.

Follow the Camptown Ladies crew when they hit the road for a much needed break in Provincetown, and for their triumphant return as they build what could be much more than just a campground, that is, until Marie falls for the one person in the world she can't possibly have . . .

When the campfires start heating up, someone is likely to get burned . . . and the meatball could hit the fan for several members of the Santora clan!

Sequel to *Greetings From Jamaica, Wish You Were Queer.*

Paperback Original | ISBN 978-1-932859-86-7 | $14.95

Available at your local bookstore
or call 734-662-8815
or order online at www.bywaterbooks.com

Bywater Books represents the coming of age of lesbian fiction. We're committed to bringing the best of contemporary lesbian writing to a discerning readership. Our editorial team is dedicated to finding and developing outstanding voices who deliver stories you won't want to put down. That's why we sponsor the annual Bywater Prize. We love good books, just like you do.

For more information about Bywater Books and the annual Bywater Prize for Fiction, please visit our website.

www.bywaterbooks.com